I0552771

LOST AND FOUND

The Moondreams House
Romance Novels

Book Two

Ros Rendle

SAPERE
BOOKS

LOST AND FOUND

Published by Sapere Books.

20 Windermere Drive, Leeds, England, LS17 7UZ,
United Kingdom

saperebooks.com

Copyright © Ros Rendle, 2022

Ros Rendle has asserted her right to be identified as the author
of this work.
All rights reserved.

No part of this publication may be reproduced, stored in any
retrieval system, or transmitted, in any form, or by any means,
electronic, mechanical, photocopying, recording, or otherwise,
without the prior written permission of the publishers.
This book is a work of fiction. Names, characters, businesses,
organisations, places and events, other than those clearly in the
public domain, are either the product of the author's
imagination, or are used fictitiously.
Any resemblances to actual persons, living or dead, events or
locales are purely coincidental.

ISBN: 978-1-80055-845-8

PROLOGUE

Maggie placed the plastic bag on the bed. It had orange, red and brown stripes and gaped accusingly. If she was caught leaving it, she might be given long-term accommodation in one of Her Majesty's correction centres.

At first, she ignored the sound of blood pumping in her ears. This had to be done. She picked up the yellow blanket, holding its warmth to her face, and inhaled deeply to fasten the smell in her mind. She spread it in the bottom of the bag. Oh Lor, this was real. The sound became deafening, made her dizzy. She sat down heavily. What if she felt a weighty hand on her shoulder as she left her consignment? That was how she must think of it — not as treasure or anything that was hers to keep. Worse, if she was too late, the newsagent would already have unlocked and would be there before her, and she wouldn't be able to leave it. She slumped as she sat on the edge of the bed, wrapping her arms around her chest to still her heart. Oh, how she wanted to flee this task, to disappear. But she had no choice.

Maggie reached for the spare Babygro, the one she'd nicked. Heat crept up her neck at the memory. She took two deep breaths and thrust the tiny garment into one end of the bag. The bottle, still too hot, was wrapped in the only spare towelling nappy. That had been pinched too. She remembered looking around before swiping it, then tucking it down her jeans and pulling her coat as far over her expanding belly as she was able.

She felt the dryness in her mouth again now and wiped her clammy hands down the sides of those same jeans. She thought she might pass out. One more thing. She stood over the helpless child. With a watery smile, she picked her up, warm and heavy in her hands. The last thing to go into the bag.

She thought back to the fateful day when all her serious troubles had begun.

CHAPTER 1

2009

"Dad, where's my application form?" Natalie shouted. "Is it in your desk drawer? Dad?" On getting no reply, she decided he might be in the garden. It was a fine, sunny Saturday, so that was most likely. She went on to the landing and peered out through the narrow window. Yes, there he was, with his head down and his backside in the air as he pulled weeds from the tiny flowerbed. Natalie opened the window and called, "Dad, do you think my form for that job will be in your desk drawer? I've decided to go with it."

William righted himself and, pink in the face, gave her a thumbs-up. He wiped his forehead. "I think I stuck it in there when I found it on the table last week. You were at your dance lesson."

Natalie sighed. He'd always been pernickety. "Okay if I dig it out? I need to get on with it."

He gave her another thumbs-up and returned to his task.

It was great that she'd been able to come back to live with him when her life had begun falling apart, but now she needed her own place again. Despite it being nearly a year since she'd moved back in, half her stuff was still in boxes, though she had melded back into her dad's routines. He automatically tidied up after her. There was no way she'd go to her mum's and stepfather's house again, even though they were on reasonable terms now.

She went into the tiny office and pulled the drawer, tucking her long, blonde hair behind her ear. While everything was neat, it was very full, and the fold of papers was not obvious at first sight.

I wonder if it's got stuck and fallen down the back, thought Natalie. *I'm going to have to pull the drawer right out.*

She knelt on the carpet and put her hand up into the frame of the desk. She didn't find what she was looking for, but something was lurking at the back as her fingertips searched. Curious, Natalie slid out a flimsy piece of paper. It was a cutting from a newspaper, doubled over. Sidetracked from her search, she sat back on her heels and unfolded it. The paper was fragile and yellowed with age, but still legible:

In the early hours of the morning on a cold December day, imagine a young woman who must have sloped past a doorway, casting her eyes back and forth before looking over her shoulder. Then she would turn, probably with haste. Finally, she left her striped, plastic shopping bag in the small shop entrance, before hurrying away.

Alex, 65, who opened the bag before unlocking his newsagent shop early that morning said, "I had the surprise of my life. I heard this mewling noise. Thought it was a kitten or something. The baby girl was dressed nice, like, and wrapped in a yellow blanket. There was a note with her that ended: 'I'm so, so desperately sorry.' There was a bottle of milk wrapped in a towelling nappy as well. It was still warm, and there was a change of Babygro."

"I'd say she was clearly loved," Mr Adair, son of the owner said. "It was all very tender."

Natalie turned the paper over and back before re-reading the article. It was from 1985. She'd been born about then — as an adoptee, she didn't know her exact birthday, but celebrated it on January 10th. The article was twenty-four years old, and an odd thing for a man like her dad to keep. He had moved into the house when he and her mum had split up — Natalie had been three — and everything had had to be sorted or thrown away. She carefully re-folded the article and tucked it under a pad of post-it notes. After another dig around, she found what she was really looking for and returned downstairs to sit at the kitchen table.

William pushed open the door with his elbow and went to the sink to scrub his hands and nails clean. "What are you up to then, love?"

"I've decided to leave the care home once and for all and apply to the bistro I showed you the other day."

"I guess the home's been okay as a stop-gap, but you did all that catering training, so you should be working somewhere with a bit more scope." William nodded at the papers. "That place isn't too far to travel at night after you've finished a late shift."

"That's it. I must get back on the horse, as they say."

"It's not the work, though, is it?" William went on. "You were unlucky with that boss trying it on all the time. Then the stalking…"

"Mmm."

"Well, he paid the right price when the police got involved. You're well out of it all."

"I know. I've been safe here."

"And now you're with Stephen. He's a gentle, kind sort of man.. Are you dancing later?"

"Yes, he texted me, so we'll meet at Moondreams House. May go for a drink after. The later class have started to join us at the pub, so it should be quite a crowd."

"The dance school seems to be really taking off."

"Seems like it. Annie's worked so hard to keep it going. It's growing at last. I enjoy it. Are you sure you don't want to come? We made quite a passable stab at it when we went to that tea dance that Annie organised," Natalie said.

"I'm going to the photography group tonight, remember?"

"You don't mind me going with Stephen?"

"Dear girl, of course not. It's not a good evening for me anyway, like I say. I know we started off together, but it's right that you go off and find your own friends, especially after what happened. You cut yourself off a bit then. I understand why you wanted a clean break, but…"

"Mmm. The only friends I had were involved with that care home, so I didn't really want to see any of them." Natalie's chair scraped the tiles as she stood, then she gave her dad a quick peck on his roughened cheek. "Love you, Dad."

"Go on with you. Get that letter written and fill in that application." He nodded at the laptop on the table. "I'm going up to get showered and changed."

The people from the dance class had rearranged the tables and stools in the backroom of the pub in the village. It was scruffy but handy, since Moondreams House — the Georgian mansion where the classes took place — was nearby. There were shiny stains and bald patches on the ancient carpet, and the tables could have done with a sanding and re-varnishing. They were all covered with pale rings and scratches. The class had the use of this room to themselves, though, and any noise from the television or the lads around the dartboard was muffled.

"That was a good workout tonight," Christine, one of the older ladies said. "Cha-cha-cha and rock and roll."

"Good for us all," her husband James agreed, placing his hand on the small of her back. "I quite like that new waltz sequence Annie started us on."

He never used to touch her with love, Natalie thought as she looked around the group. She must ask Stephen about them later. She'd ask him about Edith, too. She looked across at the lady who could have come from another era, with her old-fashioned pleated skirt, nylon blouse and cardigan. Her jolly manner would grate on some, but she was well-liked here now that people had got to know her better. Natalie wondered if she'd known David Troughton, the owner of Moondreams House, before she'd started partnering him in class. They were of a similar age.

Conversation whirled around her as she glanced sideways at Stephen. He really was beguiling. Warmth and well-being ran through her as she looked at his profile. He laughed, and she knew his grey eyes would be sparkling. The dimple appeared in his cheek, where dark stubble grew. It had grazed her chin earlier when he'd kissed her as she'd entered the ballroom of Moondreams House.

Perhaps things were looking up again at last. A little shiver ran through her as Natalie remembered her old life. It made her feel vulnerable. Once she'd been confident and eager, but now she was careful and contemplative. She needed to grab the opportunities that were presenting themselves and move on, but it was hard when her trust had been broken so severely.

Then, images of the strange newspaper clipping entered her head. How strange to be left as a baby, defenceless and alone. Another shiver ran down her spine. For the very first time, she began to wonder about her own birth parents.

The warmth of Stephen's touch on her arm dragged her back to the present. "Another drink?" he asked.

CHAPTER 2

1984

Maggie looked towards the woods as she walked. They seemed to summon her on this blisteringly hot day. The sun was relentless, and the path she trod was crumbly and dry. The coolness beneath the trees would be welcome. The petrichor, after the dry dusty aroma of the fields and farm track would be delightful, peaceful, soothing and what her soul craved. She hoped to be the only person there — surely it was too hot for anyone else. At the division in the path, she turned and headed that way.

The last time she'd spoken with her therapist, she'd been told to take daily exercise. The medication and endless talking had helped ease the out-of-body mindset and her indifference to her future. She didn't cry all the time anymore, so she supposed she was getting better. She was on her own — that was the problem. Sometimes she needed someone to tell her what to do or to listen to her worries.

Glancing to one side, she saw movement. A flash of colour, and then it was gone, shielded by the trees — but then she saw it again. Blue-grey and dusky pink. A jogger. Oh no. At this rate, they would meet at the little wooden bridge that would take her across the drainage ditch and into the shade of the trees beyond. Perhaps if she slowed, the person would have passed by the time she got there.

As she strolled, the runner re-emerged and stopped. He bent over, presumably to ease his breathing. This was not going well. Then he straightened and began stretching, using the handrail on the bridge as support. Maggie dithered before deciding. There was nothing for it but to carry on. She'd look unstable and feeble if she turned on her heel and returned the way she'd come, and she'd spent months trying to prove she wasn't either of those. Hopefully, the runner would step aside, and she could pass into the welcome shade.

As she reached the bridge, he straightened up. Maggie hesitated, for there before her was the most devastatingly good-looking man she had seen in a long while. He was older than she, but still in his middle years, she guessed. His hair was attractively grey above his ears, while still retaining the dark streaks of his youth. As he became aware of her, his head jerked, and his fingers reached to pinch the bridge of his nose. In impatience or deliberation? Maggie's insecurities came to the fore. After a moment of more dithering, she sighed and stepped forward again with renewed determination. It was his eyes that were the most stunning thing about him. The colour of slate, they grew wide with surprise as they regarded her.

"I'm sorry, did I startle you?" Maggie forced a smile.

The jogger's eyes darted away, and he shrugged. "I didn't hear you coming, is all." He glanced sideways at her before looking somewhere over her right shoulder. "No problem."

"It's so hot out there." Maggie tossed her head back to the way she had come, and her blonde hair flew behind her.

"Do you often come this way?" the jogger asked. "I haven't seen you before, and I run through here most days. It's so cool and well…" He shrugged again as his eyes slid away.

Not brash, then, Maggie thought. *The best sort.* She'd had enough of over-confident men. As she regarded him, she marvelled that, although he had been exercising hard, he wasn't sweaty. He stood a head taller than she, and he had the classic broad shoulders and long legs of a sportsman. Good legs, too.

Maggie experienced a shiver somewhere deep inside and raised her eyes again.

"I was going to walk along this path inside the wood," she said. "It's too hot to follow the edge of the field, and it goes the same way."

"That's the way I'm going. Do you mind if I walk with you?" the good-looking man asked.

Maggie hesitated. She didn't want company, but she was trapped, now. This was a quiet spot. No one else was around. She didn't want to appear rude but… Well, plenty of dog walkers did come this way, and she had a whistle and the pepper spray. Her hand slid into her pocket and around it, taking comfort.

"You'll be safe. I'm not a mass murderer. It's only a couple I've done away with." The man chuckled, and his smile dimpled his cheek above the dark stubble. "My name's Jay, by the way. Like the bird."

"And I'm Maggie." She took a deep breath. "I love the earthy smell of it here, especially on a day like this. Even the birds are singing somewhere up there. They're all hiding from the sun over the fields. There's not even a skylark out there. It's too hot for them." Maggie was aware she was gabbling. She managed to still her chatter and they walked in silence for a minute or two before resuming their small talk.

A dog walker passed, going the opposite way. Maggie's breathing calmed as they followed the winding path, and Jay didn't appear to be too intrusive. They came to the edge of the woods. "This is where I turn back," she said.

"And I cross the field out there and head for the village," Jay said. "Thank you for your company." There followed an awkward moment of silence before Jay took a deep breath and added, "I've enjoyed our chat." He looked at his feet and scuffed the soft earth at the edge of the wood.

"Me too. Thank you," Maggie said.

"Look," he continued, avoiding her eyes, "do you fancy coming for a drink this evening? It's going to be warm. We could sit in the garden at the Red Lion. I take it you know Manderthorpe?" He nodded at the village. "I promise, I'll have showered by then." The dimple re-appeared.

"That would be lovely," Maggie said. "I'll meet you there." They arranged a time.

Mutually reluctant for the evening to end, Maggie and Jay lingered over the last dregs of their drinks, chatting about anything and everything. Interspersed with laughter and joy, the hours had evaporated without either of them surreptitiously glancing at watches. When it got chilly, they had moved indoors to a table for two. In the candlelight, they had continued to chatter. Maggie even found herself telling him about her parents.

At the end of their evening together, they stood in the deserted carpark, the only light from a bulb down near the pub doorway and the myriad stars above.

Maggie wanted him to kiss her. She had been so lonely. Surely this was telling her she was ready for another relationship after all this time, and he seemed so perfect. If his lips met hers, she wouldn't want him to stop. Her heart beat faster. She looked up at him, and in the gloom, his face lost focus. At that moment, he bent his head as her lips came towards his. The kiss they shared was deep.

"Oh Maggie, I can't believe such a chance meeting has brought us together. I've never been with anyone like you. Ever. You tell me you've been hurt but I would take care of you." He leaned to kiss her again and gently took the back of her head in his hand while caressing her face, his thumb softly grazing her cheek. She returned his kiss with a quiet groan of pleasure.

Maggie and Jay's friendship became a relationship before either of them knew the other well enough. A few months later, they were living together.

"I do love you, Maggie," Jay said as they lay next to each other.

She snuggled in and lay her head in the familiar crook of his shoulder as his arms came around her. "And I love you. I'm so glad we met each other that day."

Jay took her hands and raised them over her head, pinning them there, holding her wrists as he rolled on top and kissed her. She wriggled. She would have preferred to have her arms around him, but he liked to be masterful in bed. That was alright. He knew how to satisfy her in the end.

He leant away and reached for something. Before she understood what was happening, he had wrapped one of his neck ties around her wrists and looped it to the railed bedhead.

"Jay, I'm not sure about this," she whispered.

"Shh! Let me show you." He began kissing her neck and then moved down.

There was no doubt he knew how to pleasure her, but she couldn't help being tense. She was vulnerable and helpless like this.

He came to his climax quickly when the moment arrived. She knew how to pretend. Then he rolled off, reached up to untie her and said, "Good girl. That *was* good, wasn't it?"

Things had moved fast, Maggie thought as they lay together, but it mostly felt so right. And now here they were — living the life and sharing the dream.

"Fast or what?" Maggie's close friend Harriet said. "I'm pleased for you, I am, truly. It's all moved so fast, though. You are alright, aren't you?" Then she laughed. "I can always get in touch with my old crowd."

The coffee machine behind the counter hissed and gurgled so loudly, it made Maggie start and her heart jumped. "I'm absolutely fine, and don't even joke about them. The East End was a bad place for you, and I'd *never* need that kind of service, thanks, no matter how bad things got. It's all good. When the right guy comes along, you know. It's as simple as that."

"'E's a looker, for sure."

"It's not that, though. He cares. He really does."

"I'm pleased to 'ear it. It's just that we never seem to see you these days. My mum always used to say, 'Don't give up yer old life. You never know when you might need it.'"

"That's a little pessimistic. I've been busy, is all." Maggie took a sip of the coffee, but it was too hot and she screwed up her face. She glanced surreptitiously at her watch, and a wave of heat coiled around her neck. *I'm going to be late home*, she thought. She made an effort. "Anyway, what have you been up to?"

"We had such a ripe ol' time at Casio's the other night. It's such a shame you couldn't make it. I 'ope the tummy bug wasn't too bad. It was a right old laugh. Jacky was on full form and at one point, 'alf the room stopped to watch 'er perform."

"It was a last-minute thing. Didn't last long, but it made me feel like a dishrag." Maggie wished she had been at the club with her friends, having a laugh. "Did you share a taxi? What was she wearing?"

"The pink 'alter-neck. Remember it? That alone was enough to cause a stir, never mind 'er long blonde 'air swishing around, and those boobs swinging free under the fabric. Of course, all the lads were 'aving an eyeful. She could 'ave gone off with any of 'em, but that's not 'cr thing, is it? She likes the attention, but that's all." Harriet gave her raucous laugh, but Maggie knew the kind heart beneath the brash façade. Her longing increased. She missed the girly banter and closeness of sharing.

She loved Jay. She did. He was good to her. He just didn't like them being apart. Except for work, of course. That couldn't be helped. He always said even that was too long. It was testament to his feelings for her and his need to protect, that he wanted her by his side. That was all it was. She was so lucky.

"Sorry." Maggie shook her head. "What was that?"

"I was saying, we talked about a weekend away before the summer comes. Maybe Brighton? Newquay would be good too. What do you think? Just you, me, Jacky, and Laura. We could either get a cheap 'otel for three or four nights or find a B and B. That might be better. They're such good value, and we've never minded bunking up, 'ave we?"

"I'll think about it," Maggie said, aware that she would have to think how to duck out of it. "Money's a bit tight at the mo," she said to prepare the way.

"Oh, go on. It's not for three months yet. Plenty of time to save up. It'll be such a laugh. The crowd together again."

"I'll have a think. Chat with Jay."

"You don't need 'is permission." Harriet sounded disparaging.

"Of course not. We do live together, though."

"Does 'e go out with the lads?"

"Of course. Football some Saturdays, and there's usually a thing after — in the evening, for a drink. They go all over. He can't always go, though. Once a month he goes to check up on the tenants he has in his parents' old house. He went to a stag do in Dublin last month. Only for a couple of nights. He said he didn't want to go, but he couldn't get out of it. Sounded quite a raucous do. He wouldn't mind me going. Of course not." But perhaps she was protesting and explaining too much. He wouldn't be happy, she knew it.

"There you are, then. Money won't be no object. Our outing won't involve the expense of a flight. We can car share."

"Okay. Well, leave it with me." Maggie looked at her watch. "Crikey. Look at the time. I must go."

Maggie was happy to leave the steamy café with its noisy coffee machines. She hunched her shoulders against the wind as she reached the pavement. It was supposed to be spring soon but didn't seem like it. With awkwardness, because of the plastic bag she carried as well as her handbag, she managed to pull up her collar as she ducked around the other people on the pavement. Everyone was heading home after a morning's shopping or whatever, and it was busy. Skipping into the gutter to get around a woman with a buggy, she hopped back up and skittered on towards the bus station, looking at her watch again and speeding up as a result, so that by the time she reached it she was puffing.

"I didn't know you were going out," Jay said when Maggie returned, later than she intended.

She dumped the bags on the chair by the little table in the kitchen. "No, well, Harriet rang after you left for the gym. Asked if I wanted to meet her for a coffee. I nipped into that new clothes shop before that. Let me show you. I hope you like it. I simply fell in love with the colour."

"I'm not sure I like Harriet," Jay said. "She's got a dodgy background."

"She's not seen any of them for years. How did you find that out?" Maggie wrinkled her forehead. "You sound grumpy."

He shrugged and looked over her shoulder. "I asked around after you introduced her that first time. I'm really not sure she's a good friend." Jay placed his arm around her shoulders and pulled her close. "I was worried about you," he said. "I was hoping we could go out to lunch, but we've obviously missed that."

"I'll get us a sandwich, and perhaps we could go out for a bite tomorrow," Maggie said, sounding cheery. The last thing she wanted or needed was a spikey conversation. Not when she'd had a fun morning. She had enjoyed her time out with her friend and managed to stamp down much of the disquiet during the ride home. "Look at this. What do you think?" She held a filmy peacock-blue dress against her.

"Very nice." Jay turned away and pulled the bread knife from the magnetic strip to one side of the sink. He turned back and waved it at Maggie. "You could have rung the bar at the gym when you guessed I'd be there after the workout."

She stepped back, then sighed. "I could have, but I didn't. I left a message at reception to let you know where I was and that I was okay. Please don't be like this."

"Like what?"

"Nothing. I'm sorry. What would you like in your sandwich? I've got some of that pastrami you really liked the other day."

"Fine." Jay stuck the bread knife vertically into the board before he left the room, and she heard the bathroom door close and the bath running.

For several seconds Maggie watched the handle wavering in the air before she pulled the blade out and retrieved the bread from the bin.

As she cut four slices with care to get them even as Jay preferred, her heart beat just a tiny bit faster and a small worm of discomfort slithered around in her tummy. She took a deep breath to dispel the tension. It was only because he cared for her, and what she had told Harriet was true. She was extremely fortunate to have someone who loved her so much.

He couldn't possibly object to her having a weekend away with the girls. What harm could befall her if she had their company? He would see that. Harriet was right. She shouldn't let all her long-standing friendships lapse. Over their snack she'd mention it. It would prove his love and trust in her. It sounded great. A weekend having a laugh, dancing, enjoying a drink. They'd had a blast last time. It was all innocent. Just girls letting their hair down.

As Maggie placed plates and cutlery on the little table, Jay returned. Coming through the door behind her, he slipped his arms around her waist and nuzzled her neck. "Oh, Maggie," he whispered. "You're all I have since my parents had their car accident. You're my little healer, remember?"

She turned in his arms, and bending her head back she stood on her toes and kissed him. "I know. I love you and would never do anything to upset you. It was a providential breeze that day when we met, and I know it."

They sat in silence as they munched on the sandwiches. His good humour had returned.

Maggie looked at him, and in the silence, she thought, *He's like the bird of his name. He's shy. He can be bold and … and territorial, even, but only in defending what he loves.* She was part of that now. Just when she'd needed it, he'd come into her life.

Both her own parents were gone. First the divorce and her dad moving abroad, then her mum's cancer, so sudden. What a year.

"Jay, I know your mum and dad were killed in the accident, but how did it come about? Will you tell me? We've never really discussed it."

His face became still, and his slate eyes cast down. After several seconds of silence, Maggie began to wonder if she shouldn't have asked, and some agitation returned.

"It was the brakes." He glanced at her before looking sideways out of the window at the clouds which matched his eyes. "We lived at the top of a steep hill. The car's brakes didn't work. A catastrophic leak, apparently. A damaged line. It let air into the system and the cylinder failed. I was away at a conference for a couple of days when I got the phone call. They raced down the hill into a truck going past the T-junction at the bottom. They didn't often use the car but before I left for work, they said they were going to visit one of the National Trust properties and take a picnic, so they'd have to go that way. It sounded like they'd planned a good day out, but…"

"So, you were living at home then?"

"Mmm, but as I said, I wasn't there that day." He fixed his eyes upon her. "I'd only moved back in temporarily. I'd never intended to stay as long as I did, but first one thing and then another meant I was out of work for a while. None of it was my fault. I'm truly not sure how I stuck it with them." He shrugged, that characteristic tell-tale sign of discomfort. "My dad was always at my throat. Nothing I ever did was good enough. Always something wrong. Still… In the end…" He gave a little grimace. Or was it a small smile? "I was able to buy this place because they died."

"But you still own their house."

"I wouldn't want to live there. Much better to rent it out. The life insurance helped." That small curve of his lips reappeared.

"Oh." There was nothing else to say to the revelation. Maggie shivered and watched from under her eyelashes as Jay dug his straight, white teeth into the sandwich.

"What were you and Harriet so engrossed in that it made you late?" he asked.

Here we go again, she thought. "Since you've asked," Maggie began, taking a deep breath, "she said the girls are thinking of a long weekend break. Not for two or three months. Brighton or somewhere cheap. Just a girls' trip. A bit like your stag weekend, but definitely without the riotous element. I *really* don't believe we'll do anything like you lot did. I mean, taping that guy to his bed and leaving him in his underpants with no money was a bit over the top."

"I already said, I don't like Harriet."

"That's because you don't know her properly. She was so good to me when I had that break-up before. She let me stay at her place rent-free and took great care of me. Honestly, she's lovely."

"I don't see why you want to go off on some wild outing. I was planning to take you for a romantic weekend away. We could hire a cosy cottage, eat at a lovely pub I know in the Peak District, take walks … together."

"Oh, Jay, that sounds perfect. I could do both, though. The girls' weekend would only mean taking one day off work, and I have loads of leave left."

"It sounds dreadful. Brighton? Really! You're not a student anymore." He pushed his chair back, and the legs scraped the tiles violently. "Don't you love me? Is that it? I'm not enough for you?" He went and stood by the sink, his back to her.

Maggie pushed her chair back, too, and quietly stood beside him. After a moment of hesitation, she put her arm around his shoulders. "Oh, Jay. You're my world. Surely you know that."

"And you are all I have since my parents' car crash. You know that, yet you punish me by talking of going away." He hung his head and sounded so mournful that Maggie leant against his shoulder.

"I won't go. It's not that important, Jay. I love you. I do. I'll phone Harriet right away and tell her we're busy around then. Well, we will be, won't we, if you have a weekend planned? That sounds so great. You are good to me."

Maggie didn't have to wait long before Harriet answered. After the preliminary greetings, she said, "It's a no-go for the girls' trip. Sorry."

"Why not? What on earth's the problem?"

Maggie explained that Jay had planned a romantic weekend for them.

"Surely you could do both." Maggie heard the sigh at the other end of the line. "Maggie, I'm worried for you."

"Don't be daft," Maggie said, but again she felt a sliver of disquiet slide into her throat. She swallowed.

CHAPTER 3

Natalie sat to change her shoes at the end of the dance lesson at Moondreams House the following week. Annie asked her students if any might stay on for ten minutes so that, with those who had arrived for the next class, she might speak to them all about another social dance she was hoping to arrange. She dragged a chair and sat, inviting the others to do the same.

"I know I'm only four months gone," she said, placing a hand over her stomach with a self-conscious look, "but I'm no spring chicken to be having another child." She smiled when they all demurred.

"You need to take the weight off your feet when you can," Christine said. "I know ours were ages ago," she added, glancing across at James, "but I remember how tired I got." Her husband looked at her with a tiny frown. She shook her head. Sometimes he still criticised, but not so often these days.

"You're looking blooming, as they say," Natalie remarked. She hoped she and any future husband didn't ever get irritated by each other, she thought, looking at Christine. Still, since they'd started dancing together, Christine and James seemed much closer and he didn't often put her down anymore.

"Thanks. I'm past the sicky stage now and in that middle phase where everything's great." Annie glanced across at Harry, her partner. He had taken the opportunity between classes to pop in and make sure Annie was alright. He stood next to her now with his hand on her shoulder. Annie smiled up at him. "You don't let me do too much, do you?"

"We couldn't be better, now, could we?" He looked at her with love. "Everything seems to be going well, but we don't want to spoil it."

"So," Annie continued, "another social dance. I'm thinking we could go bigger and bolder than the first one we had."

"That one was very successful," Stephen said.

"Exactly. So, we need to build on that before the memory fades. I was thinking more of a dinner dance than a tea dance. David and I have talked it over."

"Yes," David said, "we could roll up the Turkey carpet and put tables out in the hall for dining, and the caterer can use the kitchens for anything they can't bring ready-made."

"I've started to organise a caterer. I've put feelers out and had some quotes, which are mainly realistic."

"What sort of meal and ticket price are you talking?" asked James.

Annie gave examples of the sort of three-course meal on offer and the price. "In all honesty, I have to make a small profit. It's my livelihood, but it needs to be realistic for you all to want to come, too."

Natalie's ears pricked up when Annie described the catering, and she caught Stephen's look. He gave a smile and an almost imperceptible nod. He knew she'd love to do something like that, but it was more than she could take on currently. While she was awaiting a response to her application to the bistro, she was doing extra shifts in the care home kitchens to make ends meet.

Annie continued with her thoughts for the grand dance.

Then Christine said, "So it's more like an autumn ball."

"Will it be long dresses and suits for the guys?" Natalie asked. "It would be fun to have a really dressy do."

"I've never been to anything like that," Morag said.

Mick, her boyfriend, put his hand on her knee. "You'll be fine. I'll be there. It'll be fun." She smiled up at him. Morag had really come a long way with her confidence since starting Annie's classes and meeting Mick. It was so sweet to see.

"So, what do we think?" Annie was speaking again. "It's no good if you don't all want that kind of thing. You're all my friends now, and I'll be guided by your opinion before opening it up to other groups like we did before."

It was true. Annie had helped many of them re-find themselves. In turn, Natalie thought, perhaps they had all helped Annie, too. She and Harry — childhood sweethearts — had reconnected and deeply adored each other. She'd love to be like them, she thought. Perhaps she sighed out loud, because Stephen looked across at her and whispered, "Are you okay?"

She smiled at the concern in his grey eyes. "Yes, I'm fine." He was a lovely guy, and they were good friends as well as new lovers.

There was a general consensus of approval of Annie's proposals.

As Natalie pulled on her boots, Stephen asked, "Your dad is coming for you, isn't he?"

"Yes, he'll be here. He's leaving his evening class spot on time. He knows you have to get off to work." Stephen worked shifts as a hospital porter. He loved it and he was good at it too, from what Natalie gathered.

Just at that moment, William appeared at the door to the ballroom. He carried an umbrella, but Annie opened the door for him and beckoned him inside.

"Come on in. The weather's really turning now. You'll get soaked out there in no time. Have you come for Nats, or did you want to see me? I haven't seen you for quite a while. Is everything okay?"

"I'll stay and drip onto the mat. Don't want to spoil the floor. Not after the ceiling catastrophe at the beginning of the year."

Annie smiled at the memory. "Disaster in one way, but the saviour of us all in another. At least it ensured David stepped up and got the place fixed. Look at him." She nodded across the hall to where the elderly owner of the house sat with Edith while they both changed into their outdoor shoes. "Anyway, how are you?"

"I'm fine. And I can see you are too. Keeping well and not overdoing it, I hope." William looked at her growing baby bump.

"Harry won't let me do that. You haven't really answered my question, though, William. Are you happy and busy enough?"

"Yes, I am. As you know, after the little dating debacle you and I had, I'm better off on my own. I don't need or want romance. Family and friendship are enough. I've got plenty of friends and one in particular, Pat, seems great. We see eye to eye, as it were."

Annie gave him a hug, despite his wet jacket. "I understand. Well, you know where Harry and I are at any time."

"I do, and I count myself fortunate that we met. Also, that you were so understanding." William looked sheepish and shrugged, but he kissed her cheek.

At that point, Natalie and Stephen joined them.

"Hello, darling," William said to his daughter, and he shook hands with Stephen. "Duty calls?" he said to the young man.

"'Fraid so. I really don't mind, though. I do love it at the hospital. Never two shifts the same. Thanks for coming for Nats." He placed his arm around her shoulders, and she leaned in against him.

CHAPTER 4

Life continued for Maggie and Jay. She was rarely far from him. Sometimes she thought it might be good to go to a fitness class or maybe out with Harriet for a drink and a chat, but it never seemed to happen, and time slid silently by. Then something did happen that made Maggie's fear resurface.

She was looking for a ruler. She'd already looked in the junk drawer in the kitchen and in her office bag, and now she was scouting around in the tiny third bedroom Jay used as an office. He didn't really like her poking about in here, but he was out playing football and would go for a drink with the lads after, so he wouldn't be around for ages. She needed to measure some fabric she was going to turn into a basic little cushion.

As she pulled out the small drawer, her ears were almost aching as she listened, and her heart thumped just a little bit faster than normal. Still, she'd be quick. The drawer was full of the usual paraphernalia, so she pushed her hand in deeper to feel for what she needed. There was a tickle along the back of her wrist, and she pulled it away with haste, picturing a big, black, hairy spider. But it was just a piece of paper, hanging down from the strut of the desk above. She turned her fingers and carefully pulled it out. Flimsy and slightly yellowed with age, it was a newspaper clipping folded in half and half again. She turned it over and read the headline:

COUPLE KILLED IN FREAK ACCIDENT
Strange circumstances led to husband and wife, Dot and Ben Masters being killed as their car plunged down the steep hill of Glen Road and into the path of an oncoming truck on The Drift.

Maggie, already kneeling, sat back on her heels as the breath left her lungs and her head swam. Strange circumstances? She read in the article the details of the relatively new car plunging down the road, to be mowed over by a heavily laden pantechnicon which had no chance of stopping. The thing that really spooked her was the doodle in the margin: it was a smiley face.

Tempted to screw the thing into a tiny ball, Maggie willed herself to carefully re-fold the paper, before she reached into the back of the drawer to hide it away under a small pad of paper. Her hand trembled as she withdrew it and pushed the drawer closed. All thoughts of the task she had planned flew away. Her knees were weak as she held the banister rail tightly and descended the stairs. Finding the sofa, she collapsed into the corner, drew her knees up and clutched her legs as she tried to control her breathing.

That evening, Maggie's panic resurged from time to time. Twice Jay asked her if she was alright. She passed it off as overtiredness and went to bed early, deciding that she would phone Harriet from work on Monday.

CHAPTER 5

Natalie was tidying up after her shift in the kitchen at the care home, when her phone rang. It was her last week, and her mind was on the new job at the restaurant as she wiped and tidied with mechanical precision. She retrieved her bag from the tiny cupboard and answered.

"Is that Natalie?" the voice at the other end asked before she had time to say anything.

"Hello?"

"Sorry, it's Annie. Stephen suggested I phone you. I've got a bit of a crisis."

"Oh dear, fire away."

"The caterer for the autumn ball has pulled out. Completely let me down. I've already sold over fifty pairs of tickets. Stephen said you were in catering. I had no idea, or I'd have spoken to you ages ago. Stephen said you were about to start work in at that hotel's new bistro place, The Wild Thyme? I wouldn't bother you, but I'm so worried."

"I could ask around and see if anyone knows of anyone else."

"Well … Natalie, in all honesty, I was hoping and praying you might consider doing it yourself. I gather you'd be more than capable. You can use the kitchens at the house, maybe keep it simple with a pre-prepared starter and dessert. You'd need help, I suppose. The girls who served at the last dance would come, I'm sure. One was the daughter of a particularly good friend, and her friend. They were very capable."

"It's daunting. I have done something similar in the past, but not for quite a while."

"If there's even a small chance… Why don't you meet me at Moondreams House, and we could have a look at the facilities in the kitchens together and chat about it? Please say you'll come and consider it."

"Okay. Right."

They arranged to meet the next day.

After Natalie finished the call, she stood for several moments. What had she done? She was about to start a new job, for goodness' sake. Still, it wasn't beyond her capabilities to come up with a simple menu. There was the thing with asparagus, cream cheese, sweet chilli sauce and prosciutto. It looked classy but was quick and easy to produce. A vegetable soup, of course, was a cheap alternative and would suit any vegetarian people. Desserts could be a chocolate mousse, an individual pavlova, the usual things. All easy to do before the event. She wondered what dishes they had at Moondreams. She was sure, when Annie did the dance before, the cups and saucers and plates were all there from back in the day when David used to run the ballroom with his late wife.

Later that evening, after a satisfying bottle of wine Natalie was sitting on Stephen's sofa in his tiny flat. His arm was around her and they were discussing the catering possibilities. He kissed her cheek. "I have every confidence you can do whatever you want. You are talented, hard-working and —" he leaned in to kiss her more thoroughly — "beautiful, and…" He kissed her again. "I think we should finish this discussion in another room." His cheeky grin won her over — not that she needed much persuasion.

As she stood in the bedroom, he unbuttoned her blouse and slowly slid it from her shoulders. With tender care, he stroked her face with one hand while the other came around her shoulders as he repeated the kiss. Natalie responded. She loved this gentleness in him, and after her previous experience it was satisfying and erotic. She encircled his body with her own arms and her back arched. She giggled.

"What?" He smiled.

"Nothing." Was it a nervous laugh? *Perhaps I'm worried something will go wrong*, she thought. "I'm just so happy. Everything seems to be falling the right way, now."

He let her go and crossed his arms to remove his T-shirt. The sight of his torso, still slightly tanned from last summer's sun, aroused her more. Her inhibitions were flying away.

Stephen lowered the zip on her skirt, and she stepped out. His hands caressed her, and she removed her underwear as deftly as she could while he removed his trousers. Then, they stood together, as close as two people could. His kisses became more powerful and urgent, and she was happy to respond.

Afterwards, they lay entwined in each other's arms. Natalie was so pleased that Stephen didn't roll over and sleep. She needed this gentle coming down from their climax of loving. He kissed her ear. "You know I'll support this thing for Annie's ball, however I can. I might be rubbish at arranging food, but I can transport stuff in the van, peel and chop, or whatever."

"Thank you. That means a huge amount."

She lay listening to the flat as it cooled and settled. She was safe here.

By the morning, Natalie was restless. A bubble of expectation was building and rising in her chest. When she arrived at Moondreams House to look at the kitchen, Annie said, "I'm so, so grateful and pleased to see you."

"I really need to see what's available here, before I can say I'll do the job." Natalie tried to put a brake on Annie's enthusiasm, although her own was barely concealed.

The kitchen was old but serviceable and extremely clean. The range had a double oven. The table was ancient, too, and had ring marks, but it was heavy, old oak and huge. Annie opened the white-painted floor-to-ceiling cupboards on either side of the enormous fireplace in which the range was housed. Natalie gasped. There were plates of every size, cups and saucers, gravy boats and serving dishes — everything she could have wished for.

"What about cutlery?"

Annie pulled open cupboards and drawers on the other side of the room. Again, it was all there.

"The biggest issue for me now is fridge space," Natalie said. She moved across and pulled open the fridge door. It was sizeable but not enough on its own.

"There's a boot room through here. Let's check it out." Annie went through a door and Natalie followed.

Only a small window lit the space. On one side was a row of pegs with old coats and hats. Underneath and up one side was an ancient-looking wooden rack, but only one pair of brogue-like shoes and two pairs of wellies occupied the space. Under the window was a huge Belfast sink and enamel draining board, and in a corner was a paper sack, presumably full of potatoes.

Leaning against the wall, beside the door they had come through, was one of the largest fridges Natalie had ever seen. The door was ajar, and the flex was coiled around the handle. It was clearly old. She imagined black mould on the inside and sparks flying when it was plugged in, but when she looked inside it was pristine and sparklingly fresh. She nodded towards it. "What do you think?"

Annie said, "Let's give it a try."

"Not you. If one of us is going to be flung across the room, it better be me."

"Hang on. Let me find Harry and ask him what's best to do." Annie left the room.

Natalie pulled the fridge door wider and was pleased to see that the plastic around the rungs showed no rust. All she needed to know now was whether it would work safely.

CHAPTER 6

Natalie couldn't get the old slip of newspaper out of her mind. The puzzle of why it was still at the back of her dad's drawer after all this time was haunting her, and she was still thinking of her own birth parents. She hadn't given them too much thought before. Despite her adoptive mum and dad separating when she was little, her upbringing with her mother had been happy, and she had never questioned her roots. Her mother had remarried when she was eight. She had stayed with her mother and stepfather for most of her childhood, seeing her dad regularly, but had decided to move in with her father for her teenage years, when, at that awkward age, she had found her mother's new circumstances increasingly embarrassing and irritating.

Natalie saw her mother regularly and got on well enough with Dennis, her stepfather. Marion and Dennis seemed to have a good marriage, and now that Natalie was older, she understood why her mother had left her dad. By his own admission, William was unable to engage in the physical side of the marriage and now realised that he was asexual.

"I've been wondering about my birth parents recently," Natalie said to Stephen as they were changing out of their dance shoes after that week's class.

"Ask your parents, I suppose," Stephen said.

"I'm not sure I can."

"Why not?"

"I don't want them to think it's not enough or they've let me down. I'm scared they might be hurt."

"Hm, I see what you mean. Should I sound your dad out somehow?"

"No, I don't think so, but thanks anyway."

As she sat opposite William before bedtime that evening, Natalie was fidgeting. She couldn't settle.

"You alright, love?" William asked. "You're restless. Are you worried about anything? What about this catering for Annie? You're not taking on too much, are you?"

"No. I'm excited about that. I've got the menus drawn up and I've done the costings. I should make something out of it as well as Annie making a bit of profit. It seems like it's going to be okay."

"Well, that's great. You're saving Annie's bacon, as they say. She was in a right fix, being let down like that. And how about The Wild Thyme? How was your meeting with the catering manager?"

"She seems great. I think we're going to get on really well. She liked my ideas for menus there, too. I suggested trying some new aperitif nibbles, canapé type things, for people who are waiting for their table. She seemed impressed with my costings, and I persuaded her it would be an advantage without being pricey."

"Well done. That's my girl." He paused and turned a page in his book. "So, what is it?" he asked eventually.

"Nothing." She got up. "I'm off to bed. Love you." She bent to kiss his cheek. The familiar smell of him and the feel of his rough cheek comforted her. As she climbed the stairs, she wondered how best to start searching for a birth parent without upsetting her dad.

Eventually, she came to a decision. After work, she would go to see her mum. She'd be finished at four, and Marion would be home by five. She'd text her dad and let him know where she was — he still worried about her.

As Natalie walked from the bus-stop the following day, she was tired. Her shift had been full-on and she was still stressed about the new canapés. She wondered if this visit to Marion's house was a good idea. She arrived outside and seeing that her mum's car was not yet in the driveway, she felt relief and prepared to walk on to the next stop to catch the bus home. Another day would do just as well — or maybe not at all. She didn't need to know anything. She was happy.

Before she could leave, the front door opened and Dennis waved at her. This was it, then.

"It's nice to see you," he said as he spooned coffee granules into two mugs after he'd insisted on hanging her coat up in the cupboard under the stairs. Definitely no quick getaway, then.

"It's been a while. I'm sorry."

"You're busy, I'm sure. Your mum will be pleased, though."

"Yeah, I know." There was a silence. Natalie searched for something to say. "How's the business going? Times are hard since the crash, I suppose."

"That's true, they are. We're not selling much, but house lets have taken off. We've got into the maintenance of those, so we're getting by. How's it with you? Did you go for that hotel bistro job?"

"Yes. I hesitated, but I started about ten days ago. It's good — so far, anyway."

"Good for you. Here." Dennis handed her a coffee as the front door opened. "That'll be your mum. I'll leave you two to have a natter. I've stuff to be getting on with."

Marion dropped her bag by the radiator and gave Natalie an exuberant hug. "Lovely to see you, darling."

Natalie made herself smile as they separated. Conversation was stilted as thoughts whirled through her mind. She had to concentrate to answer questions about her new job and to nod at the right times when Marion told her about this and that. How would she introduce the subject of why she was really there?

"Let's go through to the sitting room. You must tell me all about working at The Wild Thyme. Perhaps Dennis and I could come to eat one evening. You must let me know when you'll be working there."

Natalie sat, and the big squashy armchair swallowed her up. She tried to manoeuvre one of the cushions behind her back, so she was more upright. She looked around at the large, flat-screen TV and the glass and chrome coffee table. All very smart and modern, but it wasn't home.

"You're a bit tense, love. Is everything alright?"

Natalie took a deep breath. "I wanted to ask you something. The thing is…"

"What is it? Spit it out," Marion said and leaned forwards.

"The thing is … well … I've been wondering about my birth parents. I mean, it's not such a surprise, is it? Most adopted children wonder, don't they?"

"Yes, I guess they do," Marion said but offered nothing further for several moments. "Have you spoken to your Dad?"

"No, I haven't. I thought you might tell me. The thing is, I don't want him to think I'm unhappy. I was worried about hurting his feelings."

Marion lowered her gaze. "But not mine." It was barely audible.

"Oh, Marion, it's not that." Natalie was contrite. "Honestly, I didn't think you'd mind."

"Honey, it's fine." Her mother tossed her fringe from her eyes. "Look, I really think you ought to speak to William. It's complicated."

"What do you mean, complicated? I'm sure this sort of situation is always involved and often tortuous. I've thought about it. I know the pitfalls if I found my birth parents, and I'd be sensitive about it. If they didn't want to know me … well, fine. At least I'd know."

Marion sighed. "Yes, these things always are complicated. Have you really considered it from the point of view of them, though? They might not want to be found. You could stir up all sorts. What good would it serve? You've been happy, haven't you?"

Natalie began to feel exasperated. "Of course I've been happy. I just would like to know and yes, I've considered all of those things, like I said."

"Darling, you need to talk to your dad. He has all the information. I have nothing here, anyway. Now, would you like to stay for dinner? I'm sure we can rustle something up."

"No. Thanks, though. I told Dad I'd be back."

"You could ring him." Her tone was pleading.

This was partly why Natalie found it so hard to visit. It was never enough. Marion always wanted more and after all the years of difficulty, Natalie couldn't give more. Not yet, anyway. "I'd like to spend longer, truly, I would. Maybe next time. I promise not to leave it so long."

"Right, well, Dennis will give you a lift home. The bus will be quite full at this time of night."

"I don't mind the bus," Natalie said.

"Don't be daft." Marion stood and shouted up the stairs. "Dennis, you'll give Natalie a lift home, won't you?" Then turning back, she went on, "There, I'll get your coat. I'm sorry I can't help more with … you know. What you asked. Speak to your dad. Love you, honey."

The journey home wasn't long, and Dennis chattered most of the way. "Come again soon, Natalie," he said as she climbed out of the car. "Your mum loves to see you."

CHAPTER 7

Monday morning finally arrived after another night of sleeplessness. Maggie had desperately tried to lie still so she didn't wake Jay. When she arrived at work, there were the usual mundane tasks that had to be completed before she was able to phone Harriet.

"Hi, it's me," she said.

"You okay?" Harriet asked immediately. "It's not like you to be phoning me from work in the middle of the morning."

"I'm fine." Maggie took a deep breath. "Well, I'm not sure. There's something I need to talk to you about."

"We can meet after work, if you like. 'Ave a drink?"

"The thing is … well…"

"What's up, Maggie?"

Maggie could hear the concern in her friend's voice. "Can we meet at lunchtime? I'll explain then. I know it'll be a push, but I can't really do after work."

Maggie heard the sigh at the other end of the line. "Okay," Harriet said. "Maggie, what's all this about?"

"I'll explain when I see you. It won't take long. I can't be long." Maggie was having doubts about this course of action. Was she being silly? Over-imaginative? They arranged a time and place, and Maggie replaced the receiver the right way around on the cradle, with the wire untangled and lying neatly across the front of the phone. Even here at work the habit of leaving it as Jay preferred was ingrained, and she suddenly realised with a small shudder that she did it without thinking. She spent the rest of the morning wondering whether to phone

Harriet back and say she couldn't make it after all. Perhaps her imagination was running away, and all was fine.

At midday, she grabbed her bag and coat and ran down the stairs before exiting the office block through the rotating door. With a quick and guilty glance around, she hurried to the coffee place in the town centre where she had agreed to meet Harriet. Her friend was there before her as she threw herself into a chair at a small, round table. Harriet had already bought them each a coffee.

"Ooh, thanks," Maggie said as she let out her pent-up breath and tried to relax. Again, her eyes darted around. What if she were seen? What if Jay had decided to have a wander around the shops during his lunch break? It would be unlikely. He always said he was so busy all day, that he hardly had time to grab a bite at his desk.

"So, what's all this about?" Harriet asked. "You don't look too good. You're not ill, are you? It's not that?"

"No." Maggie took a deep breath. Her words finally tumbled out as she told Harriet about the death of Jay's parents and the newspaper clipping. "It sounds pathetic now I've told you. It's just… The doodle at the side. The weird smirk he gave when he said he was able to buy his place after they died, and…"

"Do you feel safe?" Harriet went straight to the nub of the matter.

"I think that's it. I'm not sure. We had words a few weeks ago. About this girls' trip in a couple of months. You know."

Harriet said nothing, and after a moment Maggie resumed.

"He waved the bread knife at me and then rammed it into the board with such force. It quite shook me." She sat and thought for a moment. "I don't know, Harriet. It all sounds a bit meagre and pitiful. I'm being stupid and fanciful. Look, forget I said anything. *Please* don't mention this to anyone else. You won't, will you?"

"Of course I won't if you don't want me to, but are you sure you don't want to do anything? You know you can 'ave your old bedroom at any time."

"I'm fine. Forget it. I'm being stupid."

As Maggie hurried back to her office, she glanced around nervously. At one point her heart nearly leapt out of her mouth as a car similar to Jay's pulled out of a parking space across the road, but the driver was a woman with a ponytail. Maggie chastised herself for being over-imaginative. She had a disquieting feeling of being watched, but it must have been all in her mind.

The days passed with nothing remarkable other than that same persistent sense of being followed. One lunchtime, Maggie nipped to the chemist for some paracetamol. Her lack of sleep meant her head was aching yet again. Who was that man over there with eyes following her as she crossed the road? He was Jay's age, she guessed. A beard and the same dark hair streaked with grey. When she came out of the chemist, he hobbled to one side as if he had a problem walking, avoiding her eyes before crossing the threshold himself. Another time, she saw a man who had the same Barbour jacket down the road. He turned to look in a shop window as she left the office building. He was concentrating on what was in front of him, and was clearly favouring one leg. She was tempted to accost him and ask him if he was following her, before realising she could be accused of being totally irrational.

She was frightened again the following week. Jay's car was collected from the house by the garage for its annual service, so she dropped him off at his work and he told her he'd get a lift home. Then they would go together to the garage to collect his car. As she stood by the window, waiting, he arrived home and clambered out of a car she had seen once before. Surely it was the same car that had been driven by the woman with a ponytail? Her breath left her body in a rush, and she had to steady herself against the window frame when she saw the man in the driving seat. She recognised him straight away. She could see the silhouette of his beard and the Barbour jacket with epaulettes.

With determination, Maggie glued on a smile and greeted Jay at the front door. "Who was that giving you a lift?"

"Just a guy I know from football. He does some of the groundwork, but his main job is just around the corner from me. He lives in those terraced houses not far from here."

"I thought I'd seen him somewhere," Maggie said, trying to sound nonchalant.

"I doubt it. I haven't seen him at footie for a while. He's been off with a tendon problem."

So, this was the man she had seen around so frequently. He didn't work or live near her offices, yet he had been there so many times. Was he watching and following her?

"He's a friend, though?"

"What's this? An inquisition? He's just a guy who does some odd jobs sometimes. Are we going to get my car?"

They drove to the garage in silence. "What's up with you now?" Jay said.

"Nothing at all," Maggie said.

"Did you get something from the chemist for these headaches?"

Maggie managed not to stare at Jay. He knew she'd been to the chemist. The guy she kept seeing was watching and reporting back. Or was he?

Jay continued, oblivious to Maggie's shock. "I was thinking. I'm doing well at work. I've got a new account and should be getting a bonus as well as my increase in salary from the promotion."

"You're really doing well."

"You could give up work. We don't need your money. You could relax without having to dash out during your lunch break for whatever … or to see whoever."

Maggie clamped her lips together and her jaw tightened. Her knuckles showed white on the steering wheel. After a pause, she managed, "When I was ill before, the therapist said my work routine was a good thing for me."

"Yes, but that was before we met. Ages ago. You have me now."

She glanced sideways and gave a tight smile, before driving on in silence while her brain whirled.

Later that evening, while Maggie was standing at the sink, Jay came up behind her. Circling her waist with his arms, he nuzzled her neck. A few weeks ago, she would have revelled in the show of affection. Now her stomach contracted and she shrank inwardly but tried to remain as she was, desperate that he would not sense her tension.

"We could be even more cosy here if you gave up work," he said. "I'm here for you. I don't want you getting ill again like before we met. You're all I have. I do love you."

Maggie managed to turn in his arms and paste on a smile, not too brilliant, but wide enough. She had come to a decision.

CHAPTER 8

It had been two weeks since Natalie had visited Marion and Dennis, and she'd decided she had prevaricated enough.

"Dad, can we talk?" she asked as she joined William in the sitting room.

"That sounds ominous." He looked across at her and smiled. "But of course." He put down his newspaper. "You've always been able to talk about anything with me. I knew something hasn't been right, so come on, out with it."

"This might not be so simple."

"Well, we'll give it a go … together."

"I know … but … I don't want you to read anything into this. Nothing has changed for me. I'm perfectly happy. The thing is, I was wondering about my birth parents. I don't necessarily want to find them or anything. I've always thought of you as my dad. I was just thinking about it."

"Okay." William paused and appeared to be thinking. He sighed. "Wait here."

He disappeared and Natalie heard him thundering about in the bedroom. She sat on the edge of the sofa. Perhaps she should go and follow him, but he said to wait there. She cocked her head. Was he in the desk drawer, now? After several more minutes and some more crashing and thumping, she heard his footsteps coming more slowly down the stairs.

When he came back in the room, he had a brown A5 envelope and … was that the newspaper clipping?

"First things first. Things are not straightforward. It won't be easy to find what you probably want to know," he said.

Natalie became aware of the tension across her forehead, and she shifted in her seat. "Okay…"

"This was bound to happen. I know that. You better read this first." William handed her the newspaper article.

Natalie re-read it. She was familiar with this now and all the sad implications. She said nothing but looked up at her dad.

"In this envelope is your adoption certificate. We also kept a copy of your original birth certificate, though it's not a legal document anymore. The adoption one takes over from that and is the most legal thing we have." He handed her the brown envelope. "We changed your name when you came to us, too. You'll see why."

Natalie turned it over in her hands a couple of times. She drew out the folded sheets of paper. She took in a huge breath. This was a momentous thing.

"Look at that one first." William pointed at one of the papers.

Natalie unfolded it with care and started to read. It took her a moment to understand what she saw. Some headings were unfamiliar. Her eyes skipped further down the page where the heading 'INFORMANT' sat in the middle of the page. Her eyes flicked up again as she tried to make sense of all the information on the page.

"My name was Alexandra?" She gave a little nervous laugh. "Natalie's fine. It's who I am. I don't understand. It says 'father unknown'. That's fine. But 'mother unknown'? Place of birth?" She looked up at William and straight back at the piece of paper. "Shop doorway? What?" *Informant. A. Adair. Who the hell is he?* she thought. "What is this? Wait, the newspaper article mentioned an Alex, the newsagent."

"The other paper is your formal adoption certificate." William looked at her, but Natalie could not read his expression.

"What is all this?" She leapt up paced the room. She waved the certificate she was holding, while the other papers fell to the floor. "I was a foundling? That's a horrible term."

"Yes, it is. But you are my treasure. I found my treasure. We found you when we were desperate for a child. Never doubt that. Foundling is just a term. A name given to a child who is abandoned. Who knows why it happened to you?"

Natalie collapsed onto her seat again, and her shoulders slumped as she re-read the certificate. "'Mother's name — unknown. Father's name — unknown.' Why didn't she want me? How could anyone do such a thing? It's so selfish."

William came and sat on the sofa and rested his arm across her shoulders. She leaned against his warmth.

"Perhaps she had no choice. Maybe she was too young, or in an abusive relationship. Who knows? She must have been desperate."

"She may have been raped or operating as a sex-worker."

"Yes, I suppose so. There could be any number of reasons."

"It's not normal, though, is it?"

William gave her a gentle squeeze. "It doesn't necessarily mean you weren't loved."

"Mmm, maybe." Natalie refolded the pieces of paper and, without haste, she carefully put them all, including the newspaper article, back into the envelope. "I can't spend any longer on this," she said. "I don't want to think about it at the moment."

CHAPTER 9

Maggie tapped her nails as she waited for Harriet to pick up the call. "I need to take up that offer, Harriet."

"What? Of my spare room?"

"Yes. Harriet, I'm scared." Maggie explained that she'd been followed and that Jay had suggested she give up work. "I can't talk for long. I'll have the supervisor on my back if he realises this is a private call."

"Come as soon as you like."

"Saturday? Jay will either go to the gym or play football. Not sure which. I'll lay a false trail and bring all my stuff, so I don't have to go back. Harriet, you're a star."

"See you then. I wouldn't give 'im any clues, if I were you."

"I won't, and thank you. I'll try and find somewhere else as soon as I can."

"Don't worry. Perhaps we can come to some monetary arrangement this time, since you're working again, and then you'd be 'elping me out too."

"Absolutely. I'd feel better about it then."

"You'll never guess who I bumped into the other day."

"Who?" Maggie glanced at her watch.

"Billy. From back in the day? I told you about him before."

"Oh Lor', Harriet. He was a wild one. He had some shady friends, as I recall. Don't you be getting into trouble, or we'll be in a right pickle. One of us who can't cope is bad enough. Look, I've got to go. I'm getting some pointed looks from across the floor. See you Saturday. Love you lots. Mwah!"

Maggie sighed. Now that she had a plan, she relaxed. Only two days to wait. Then she began to worry again. Supposing

Jay was ill and didn't go out on Saturday? Was she really frightened of him, or was it her imagination being overactive? Perhaps she *was* becoming ill again, as Jay had suggested she might.

Over the next two days, these thoughts re-surfaced and repeated. Maggie ensured all her things were tidy and she gradually gathered her most precious items into her wardrobe and drawers, so she would be able to pack them when in a hurry to leave on Saturday morning.

Responding to Jay's advances the night before her departure was one of the most difficult things she had ever done. Mental images and techniques for relaxation she had practised in the past helped, and when they were done, he rolled over and slept. Maggie lay rigid and still, wishing the night away, pondering her decision to move in so quickly and trying to understand when her situation had changed from one of loving care to threatening suffocation. Was it something she had unintentionally triggered? And what about his parents' accident? Surely her supposition about Jay's involvement was absurd, implausible. She shouldn't have told Harriet about that.

Maggie's letter to Jay had been written the day before, so she propped it on the table before she closed the front door for the last time. He would read it and not believe that she had the courage, but she had made it clear she was not returning and that it was over. Would he leave it at that and think 'good riddance'? She didn't think he could do that. His pride wouldn't allow it. Then what?

Maggie arrived at Harriet's door, not quite believing that she had made it with all her stuff rammed into several shopping bags and a large suitcase. It had been a struggle on the bus, but she wasn't able to bring the little car she used — she couldn't afford to run it on her own. There had been no sign of the man in the Barbour coat or the car that was so similar to Jay's. She dropped her bags and reciprocated Harriet's hug. Tears stung her eyes and she stared up at the ceiling. Her relief was palpable.

"I'm such a mess. Such a rubbish person at relationships. I'm so sorry." Maggie gulped.

"You're 'ere now. 'E doesn't know where I live, I imagine."

"No. I'm sure he could find out, though, without too much difficulty. There are directories and suchlike. It's probably easy to track someone down. I'm sure he'll find me at work, and then all he has to do is follow me or get that man to do it."

"Let's not put up our umbrella until it rains. My mum used to say that. No point worrying until we need to. Jay may just accept you've gone and leave it at that."

She and Harriet shared a bottle of Sauvignon Blanc that night and then a second. They talked endlessly of Maggie's recent ordeal and the more she talked, the more convinced she became that she did indeed have something to be concerned about.

"I hope I'm not putting you in danger by being here," Maggie said, as tears threatened again.

"I can take care of meself, and people I know, well… It's enough to say, we'll be fine."

"I only want to leave him and for him to leave me alone. I don't wish him ill."

"Of course." Harriet took a swig of her wine while watching Maggie over the top of her glass. Maggie looked away.

Monday morning and Maggie was up at silly o'clock to get ready for work. She intended to be there early, but this was ridiculous.

When she arrived at the office block, she was grateful for the security guard at the door but still looked around with care. There was nothing out of the ordinary. No sign of *that* vehicle in the street opposite. No man in a familiar coat lurked. She skittered around the corner and through the revolving door before she relaxed. Letting out her breath, she realised how tense her shoulders had been.

But when she got to her desk, there was a letter propped up against the typewriter. She picked up the envelope and looked around. Then she ripped it open. Rage was boiling up inside, or was it fear? Her hands shook as she read the note:

Maggie, you're my world, my universe, my healer. I love you. What is all this? I would never hurt or upset you. Please meet me.

She ripped it up and threw it in the bin. During her coffee break, she asked the security guard, "Did you see anyone deliver a letter for me this morning?"

"No. May have been Joe. He went off shift at eight."

When she returned to her desk after going to the staff toilets at lunchtime, there was another envelope. Maggie grabbed it and started to run for the front entrance.

"Miss May!" called the supervisor.

"I'm on my lunch break." Maggie turned her head but didn't stop.

"Yes, but don't run, Miss May." The receding voice was stern. Maggie speed-walked towards the stairs.

There was no sign of anyone. She read the message:

Maggie, please meet me. I NEED you. I love you. You're all I have.

This one rested on her desk all afternoon. Each time she glanced at it, it looked at her accusingly, but she couldn't bring herself to throw it away. Each spare moment her eyes were pulled to it again like a fish to the bait. 'I NEED you. I love you. Please meet me. Please meet me'. Echoes in her head spun round and around.

She was busy throughout the day. As she left at five, again she looked around, but there was no sign of anyone or anything unusual. That in itself worried Maggie. This was all too easy. A couple of messages and that was all? Perhaps she should meet Jay. Maybe he did love her, and she was being stupid, as usual. As she sat on the bus, she re-read his last message. If she did agree to meet him, they could discuss what troubled her. Surely he would understand and be tender. She knew he could be. Surely no terrible consequence awaited.

CHAPTER 10

Natalie threw herself into work to avoid dwelling on what she had discovered. "I need to go to the cash and carry," she said to William. "Then I must go out to the farm shop. I rang and ordered a load of stuff to be collected."

"I'll take you," said William. "This is for the dance, is it?"

"Yes. It's going to be full-on for a couple of days. I shall need to use the kitchen here for the desserts. I know it'll be a squeeze…"

"We'll manage. I'm so proud of you. You've got a good job, you're doing this favour for Annie, and Stephen seems very keen. He's a nice man, too."

Natalie smiled at him. "Always so supportive. You might be wanting to kick me out after this weekend. There'll be stuff everywhere. Stephen said he'll give me a lift with things in his van after they're made, and we'll put it all in the fridges at Moondreams House. I might just ask David if I can work in his kitchen on Friday and Saturday morning."

As they drove to the cash and carry warehouse, Natalie said, "Annie's done a brilliant job with getting the dance school off the ground."

"Lucky she found David and persuaded him to let her use his ballroom."

"Lucky she met Harry again, you mean, and that he worked there." Silence reigned for several moments. "Are you ever sorry, Dad, that it didn't work out between you and Annie?" Natalie looked sideways at William, but he steadfastly watched the road. Then she saw the corner of his mouth quirk and he gave a broad smile.

"No," he said. "You know it's not in my makeup. I had a mild flirtation with an online dating site and one or two others, but…" He shrugged.

"A dating site! I didn't know that," Natalie said. "But aren't you lonely?"

"Good gracious, no. I have my job, of course, and my photography group. I get on well with Pat there. That's all company. No, I'm not lonely, love. So, if ever you want to get your own place again or move somewhere else, don't worry about me, for goodness' sake."

They arrived at the cash and carry, and the next half hour passed in a blur as they filled their trolley with food, serviettes, and pots of table glitter. Harry and Annie were in charge of decorations, but they had agreed she would buy some of the necessary items while she was there.

"This is getting exciting now," Natalie said as they loaded the car. "I'd love to be in a position to run my own business. Still, it's risky, and the bistro at the hotel is a great place to work, it seems."

"Maybe in the future," William said.

"I've certainly got enough to keep me going at the moment." As Natalie closed the boot of the car, thoughts of her birth parents flitted through her mind and a little lump gathered in her throat.

Stephen carried the last of the trays into the kitchen at Moondreams House late on Friday afternoon. "See you later," he said to Natalie.

"About ten thirty," she agreed. He kissed her goodbye and she watched him go. She knew she was extremely lucky — Stephen was so thoughtful, caring and kind. He understood her work was important.

57

Natalie couldn't help but be excited by the buzz she had created. The last tray of desserts had joined the others and they were all sitting in the huge fridge behind the door in the boot room. The little lemon mousses were decorated with a fresh raspberry and a mint leaf. There would be a light drift of icing sugar and another three raspberries with a tiny sprig of mint on each saucer when she was plating up tomorrow. The chocolate brownies would have a rosette of cream and three white and dark chocolate buttons. Not so many had ordered cheese as an alternative, but she had sourced a delicious creamy feta as well as a Ludlow Blue, which she would serve with a warmed fig jus and a fine black pepper and sea-salt wafer biscuit. It looked classy, but was simple to do and quick to serve.

Now on to the starters. The soup was incredibly easy and cheap to produce. One of the great pots would do to warm it through on the range, and once served with a swirl of crème fraiche and an artisan bread roll, it should be fine. The prosciutto and asparagus thing she was offering would go down well too. The little chickpea fritters with soy yoghurt and green chilli jam and cucumber and pea shoots salad had been surprisingly popular. It was her vegan and vegetarian alternative and easy to produce. Now all she had to do was concentrate on those mains.

Natalie had spoken to David about the meal she was proposing, and he'd said he would source the wine for her. When she had told Annie this, she was over the moon.

"I used to be so scared of him," she laughed. "It's hard to imagine that now. He's so different. Everyone's rallying around to make this ball a success."

"Take credit where it's due," Natalie said. "People are only too happy to help. You've added a lot to their lives with your dance school. Now, you go and rest up and I'll get on in here."

Left to her own devices, Natalie looked around with a flutter of excitement. The housekeeper, Mrs M, wouldn't be around at all. She never was on Fridays. That was just as well. She was lovely in her own way, but Natalie was worried that the older lady might be resentful of her taking over the place. Now she could pretend this was her kitchen for the next two days.

CHAPTER 11

Maggie pushed open the front door with her foot as Harriet came to greet her. Before she had time to drop her bag, her friend asked, "Did you see 'im today?"

"Jay? No, nor that spy of his. I had a couple of messages, though. They were left on my table at work. He sounded so upset and … and loving. Perhaps I should… Oh, I don't know."

"Don't you dare even consider feeling sorry for that slimeball."

"I was surprised he wasn't waiting outside work. I don't know if I'm relieved or sorry. I don't know what to do. It's early days yet. I need to think. Perhaps… What? What is it?" She watched as Harriet paced.

"You 'aven't seen 'im. That's because 'e's been 'ere."

"No way! Oh, Harriet, I'm so sorry. What did he say? Oh heck, what did he do? Are you alright?"

"Let's go through and I'll give you the lowdown. It was low, too."

Maggie's breath left her, and she put her hand to the wall to steady herself as she followed Harriet down the two steps and into the kitchen at the back of the house. As she involuntarily glanced across the room, she couldn't help being comforted that the deadbolt was securing the back door. Harriet poured two glasses of wine.

I must stop drinking so much, Maggie thought. "Tell me."

"I thought working from 'ome today would be great. Mmm, not so. There was a knock on the door at about ten, and without thinking I opened it. Jay was there. I was going to slam it in 'is face but then I thought, let's just get this over with. In truth, I thought I could blag my way through it and let 'im think I knew nothing about anything."

"It hasn't taken him long to find out where you live. I shouldn't have come. What happened?"

"'E started off all smiley and charming, of course. The snake. I kept 'im on the doorstep. No way was 'e coming in. Then 'e started to get rattled. 'E looked shifty, couldn't keep 'is eyes on me, kept looking sideways."

"Yes, that's a habit of his. I noticed that on the day we met, but I took it to be under-confidence."

"'E knew I was lying, but 'e had 'is little game with me. Sayin' this and that, trying to wheedle info. Then, after a few minutes, 'e went in for the kill, so to speak."

"Oh, Harriet, I'm so sorry. He didn't hurt you, did he, or anything like that?"

"Oh, no. 'E's much too clever for that. What 'e did say was interesting, though."

"What?"

"'E said…" She paused and took a deep breath, then a gulp of wine, clearly upset. "'E said, I better be careful, especially when I was driving. 'E said, and I quote, 'Old cars like yours are notoriously unsafe'."

"We have to go to the police. He's nuts. He's a maniac."

"We could do, but honestly, I don't think there's enough evidence of anything. It'd be 'is word against mine, wouldn't it? I mean, there was a full investigation when 'is parents copped it. 'E was well out of the way then, and what do we 'ave? A few suggestions. There's not even any stalking at the mo."

"He's too clever." Maggie slumped into a chair and put her head in her hands. "What shall we do? It's all my fault."

"Don't fret. It'll sort itself out in time. 'E wouldn't be daft enough to try anything serious. It'll pass."

Time did pass. Both Harriet and Maggie were watchful, but nothing happened. However, Maggie was a little perturbed as her monthly cycle was interrupted. She said nothing to Harriet. She was probably stressed out over everything that had happened. By next month, everything would have settled down and things in that department would be back to normal. When she had been ill before and had been over-anxious, strained and depressed, things had gone haywire, and she'd missed her period. It wasn't surprising that it was happening again, what with the worry of being followed, wondering if Jay was dangerous and finally leaving him.

Gradually, Maggie began to relax into the routine of her daily life, although she still found herself looking behind her and surveying the doorways around the office block where she worked. The following month came and still there was no sign of her period. Oh, well. These things took time.

Then, she went into work one day and her supervisor tossed a copy of the local paper onto her desk. "You used to know this bloke, didn't you?"

Maggie picked up the paper. There, staring back at her, were two pictures. One was Jay's handsome, smiling face, and the other was a mangled car.

A HORRIFIC ACCIDENT

At the junction of Glen Road and The Drift, Mr Jay Masters was killed in a bizarre accident almost identical to that of his parents five years before.

Mr Masters…

Maggie dropped the paper and sat back in her chair. Her breath left her body, and she was trembling. It was four long minutes before she picked it up again. The article passed in a blur, and it wasn't until the last paragraph that she began to take it in:

Because of the odd coincidence with the death of his parents, the police are investigating. It is understood they are looking at suicide, but the tenants of his parents' old home, whom Mr Masters had been visiting, said, "He seemed no different to normal and waved as he went, saying he'd see us next month."

The catastrophic failure of the brakes on such a steep hill was an accident waiting to happen.

Maggie left work early and waited in a daze in Harriet's sitting room. She didn't know whether to sit still or pace the room. She stood and rubbed the back of her neck, then spun to perch on the edge of a chair. She looked at the clock on the wall. Its tick seemed overly loud, and she wanted to snatch it down and throw it across the floor. Then she started as she heard a key in the front door lock.

Harriet entered the room and greeted Maggie with a smile. "Everything okay?"

"Have you seen this?" Maggie waved the newspaper.

"Yeah! What goes around comes around, or whatever the saying is." Harriet grinned. "'E threatened me, but 'e's the one who's copped it. I told you not to worry, an' Billy said it'd all work out when I told 'im, too. 'E's always looked out for me. These things have a way of being okay."

Maggie stared at her friend. "You've seen Billy again, after all this time?"

"I 'aven't seen 'im, no. He called," Harriet said.

Maggie took quick, shallow breaths, almost hyperventilating. She wiped her hands down the sides of her skirt. Her voice rose. "What have you done, Harriet? What? I don't believe this." The overwhelming sense of dread was making her legs tremble. She clutched her throat.

Harriet shrugged. "I 'aven't done anything, Maggie. Get a grip. We're fine and in the clear. It's a problem solved, is all. Maggie…!" She grabbed Maggie by the shoulders and gave her a little shake. "Listen to me." Harriet's face was inches from her own. "Everything's fine."

Maggie took a deep breath and tried to calm her thoughts. What about Billy? Was he involved in this?

Harriet turned and said, "I'm going to put the kettle on the gas. Do you want a brew?" She left the room.

Maggie stayed where she was for several minutes. As she tried to reason with herself, her breathing returned to normal. And although sickness bubbled up, she managed to control it. She heard the kettle whistling. Eventually she followed her friend to the kitchen and slumped onto one of the chairs at the little table and leant against the wall. She closed her eyes.

Harriet placed a mug of tea and a biscuit in front of her. "'Ere, 'ave those. It'll 'elp yer to see things straight. We 'ave nothing to worry about. In fact, you 'ave everything to be 'appy about, now. Calm down and get that down ya. We could 'ave fish 'n' chips for tea. That'd cheer you up."

The tea and biscuit helped to calm the sick feeling. Afterwards, Maggie retreated to her room for a while. She needed to think.

That night, she slept for a surprisingly long time. It was probably a mixture of relief and exhaustion. When she awoke, she was still tired, though. What was more, her stomach was churning. Not surprising, she supposed, after all that had happened and the shock of the previous day. She lay still for a few moments, hoping it would go. Then she fled to the bathroom and threw up what little food was in her stomach.

CHAPTER 12

Natalie had deliberately kept as busy as possible, not that it had been hard. Her day job was full-on, and when Friday arrived she made sure she was at Moondreams House as early as possible. She was prepping the soup when Annie entered the kitchen with Harry.

"I do hope I'm not in your way," said Natalie.

"No, not at all. I only want a piece of toast. Harry says I must have something." Annie looked at her husband with fondness.

"Absolutely," he said. "I'm not having you fainting away. I'm insisting she takes care of herself." He looked at Natalie. "How's it going?"

Natalie told him of her activities for the day. "It'll be quite full-on tomorrow, but your friend Ginny's daughter, Ellie, is coming in," she said to Annie. "I'm paying her quite well for a teen, so she's happy."

"She's great. Her mother's been my saviour before now, but no way would I trust her in the kitchen. Ellie has her head screwed on, though, and you'll find she's a real help." Annie laughed.

A couple of hours later, Natalie put the kettle on for a cup of tea before heading down the long, dark corridor from the kitchen to the hall. She was struck afresh by the contrast from the first time she had seen this room. Its square proportions were enhanced by the light from the floor-to-ceiling windows, and David had forked out for new curtains, which now hung in rich folds. As with the ballroom next door, this room had an ornate plaster rose in the centre above her head and a beautiful brass chandelier with myriad glass droplets hung on its thick chain, casting tiny rainbows around the room. While not lit at this time of day, it was still magical. Instead of the empty black cavern of the fireplace an enormous fresh flower arrangement stood framed by the surround, and it looked like the mirror had been sorted out, too, since all the dark spots had gone.

"Has David had work done to the mirror?" Natalie turned to Harry.

"Yes, apparently it was no small job. It had to be removed from its frame and the back completely cleaned and re-silvered. It cost quite a bit and, between us, I think he's looking for a new funding source now. He's spent a ton of money since he started to take an interest in the house again."

The house was returning to its original grandeur.

However, the tables were shabby. Their metal hinges looked rusty in places and there were ancient ring marks. Natalie's heart sank a little. It was important to her that this event was a success. She desperately needed her food to be appreciated and not undermined by scruffy presentation.

Harry seemed to notice her expression. "Don't worry about the look of it at the moment," he said. "Me and Mrs M checked all the table linen. David sent them to the laundry and they all look amazing now. They'll hide all these imperfections."

"This all seems fine," Natalie said. "Kettle's on, if you want a coffee."

"I'm certainly ready for that."

Natalie was shattered by the time Stephen came to collect her, but on a high with the success of her preparations.

"Tomorrow, Harry and Annie will dress the room so that I can get on with sorting out the main courses. Salmon will take no time to cook. I've only to mix the soy sauce, lime juice and honey. I can't decide whether to add a dash of sweet chilli sauce. I got some in."

Before Stephen drove her home, he turned, placed his hand on her waist and gave her a kiss. "You need to get a good night's sleep, Nats. Try not to dream about sweet chilli sauce, or whatever's going with the chicken, for that matter," he said.

"You're right. If this is to be a success, I need to be able to concentrate tomorrow. Thank you, Stephen."

"What for?"

"All your help and moral support." He was a good man. As Natalie glanced at him, warmth rose inside her and there was a tingling which caused her to shift in her seat.

"Before we start the second half," Annie said on the evening of the ball, "I'd like you to show your appreciation for our chef tonight, and her assistants, who have provided such a marvellous meal. I must tell you that Natalie stepped in at the last minute, because I was let down by the original caterer with little time to spare. I have to say, though, I'm ecstatic at what she prepared for us with no fuss and complete professionalism."

Natalie stood and glowed. Certainly, things could not have gone better. As she looked around the great room, despite the remains of a few used plates still on the tables and half empty wine glasses, it all looked remarkable. The red-padded chairs matched the curtains with their gold-fringed pelmets, and sparkling light from the chandelier, now lit, reflected off the glassware and glitter. The pristine white cloths hid the old tables, and silver, white and red balloons rose from the centre of each one.

People stood and raised glasses to Natalie before a tumultuous round of applause filled the ancient room.

After everyone had returned to the ballroom for the last few dances, Natalie made her way back to the kitchen. There was tidying up to do. She could return tomorrow to finish off, but she preferred to get it all done tonight if possible. She was tackling the pots at the large Belfast sink when her mother's voice startled her out of her reverie.

"Well done, my love. That was a resounding success." Marion came and gave her a kiss on the cheek.

"Mind your dress," Natalie said. "The last thing you need is spots of greasy water on that fabric."

"I'm in awe of you." She stood back as Natalie got on with her work.

"Thanks."

"I was talking with your father. He looks well." Marion paused.

Natalie nodded. "Mm, he's fine." She wondered if there was something else and glanced over her shoulder.

"I gather he told you. About your birth, I mean."

Ah, so that was it. The real reason she was here. "Yes."

"Are you going to do anything?"

"Do anything?" Immediately, Natalie gave herself a mental shake. It wasn't fair to be prickly with Marion.

"Yes, I mean follow it up in any way."

"I honestly haven't thought about it." Natalie, in truth, had thought about little else when her mind wasn't taken up with preparations for this evening's food. "I'll see."

Dennis arrived. "Ah, there you are," he said to his wife. "Well done, Natalie. A fabulous meal. Congratulations." He put his hand around his wife's waist. "Come on, darling, Natalie looks remarkably busy still, and we don't want to miss the Mayfair Quickstep. It's one of your favourites." He turned Marion away. "See you soon, Nats, and again, well done."

Natalie was emptying the sink ready to refill it when her dad arrived. Drying her hands on the tea towel tucked into the waistband of her whites, Natalie turned to face him.

William rushed forwards and flung his arms around her. "Wonderful," he said. "Simply amazing. Clever girl to pull all that off with so little help. I'm so proud of you."

"Dad, mind your jacket."

"Oh, stuff that. It's fine. I'm truly so, so proud."

Natalie laughed. "I do love you, Dad. It could have been bacon and eggs and you'd have said that."

"But it wasn't, and you did it. *You* did it. Everything alright with your mother? I passed her and Dennis in the corridor."

"Yes, fine. She was asking if you'd told me, you know, about my birth situation."

"Ah. Well, you don't need to think about that now. Why don't you leave this little bit? I'll help you out with it in the morning. Come and have a dance with me. Stephen will be here soon, too."

"I'm certainly not dressed for a ball, but I do fancy a dance. Let's do it." She launched the tea towel onto the table as she passed it.

William took her hand, gave it a squeeze, and led her down the corridor and through the hall. She caught the strains of familiar dance music above the general buzz of excited voices, and as they entered the magnificent Georgian ballroom, Natalie was exhilarated again by her triumph and the success of Annie's dance school.

Back in the ballroom, she received many compliments for the meal she had designed and provided. David was particularly fulsome in his praise.

"This house has come alive since Annie persuaded me to let her use the ballroom. I must say, I'm pleased she did. As for your efforts tonight, the food couldn't have been better. Isn't that right, Edith?" He addressed the old-fashioned-looking lady, in her silky flowered blouse, pleated skirt, and strings of pearls, who hung on his arm and gazed up at him as he spoke.

"Yes, indeed, David. Young Natalie, here, has added quite a bit to the success of the evening and to the life of the house."

Natalie was pleased she'd taken up ballroom and Latin dancing at a time in her life when she needed to start getting out again. Annie's school had been the ideal thing. She'd initially come with her dad but had soon met Stephen there, and William had said he was more than happy to take up something else, leaving her and Stephen to partner each other.

The Saunter Shiraz sequence dance she was sharing with William was just finishing when Stephen arrived. He'd been home to change, and as he entered, his eyes skimmed the dancers, looking for her. Her heart gave a little skip when she saw him. He was wearing a dinner jacket, and it emphasised his broad shoulders and slim hips. His blond hair was slightly mussed by the wind and touched his collar at the back. From this distance, she was able to take in his strong brows and ever-so-slightly crooked nose, which he'd broken as a child. His jawline was slightly shadowed, but not too much, and his mouth… Natalie wished she was wearing something a little more flattering than a set of chef whites. At least she'd been able to give her long, blonde waves a rake through with a brush and had given herself a squirt of her best perfume before joining the dancers.

Stephen saw her then, and as a smile lit his face Natalie's stomach flipped. Was she falling for him in a more serious way? He waved and she returned his smile. William gave her a little push in Stephen's direction.

As luck would have it, a waltz came next, and Natalie relaxed as Stephen's arm came around her back. She seemed to fit so well in his arms. The steps they had learned over the last few months came easily now and they glided around the floor together, even managing to rise and fall and sway together in the correct places. Natalie was aware of his body down the length of her own, and she tingled in all the right places. As she turned, and they progressed round the hall, Natalie returned the nods of several people she knew from Annie's school. Then she caught her mother's eyes following them around the room.

When the dance finished, Stephen took her hand, and his warm fingers curled around her own. She revelled in his touch. Everything was going so well this evening. Then she heard a voice at her shoulder.

It was Marion. "You must be Stephen."

Natalie made the introduction. "This is my mother, Stephen. My adopted mother," she added in an undertone.

Stephen was polite and smiled widely, as she knew he would. "I'm very pleased to meet you."

Marion didn't stay long but cast an appreciative glance over Stephen and winked at Natalie as she moved away. Natalie shook her head and let out a gust of air.

"Come on. One more dance before I have to go back to the kitchen?" She pulled Stephen onto the dancefloor, where they let off steam with the cha-cha-cha.

"Your mother's a good-looking woman. I take it that's her husband now." Stephen nodded at the couple as they danced.

"Yes."

As the dance finished, Stephen led Natalie to one side of the room. "I know you're not close. Do you miss having a mum around at all?"

"I haven't."

Stephen put his head on one side and looked at her.

"I really need to get back and finish tidying up," Natalie said.

"I heard that." Annie was passing as she did the rounds from one table to another, chatting here, greeting there. "Leave the rest until the morning. We'll do the tables in the hall, and I bet there's not much left in the kitchen."

Natalie and Stephen planned to return by ten the next morning. "You don't need to, really you don't," she said to him as they climbed into his van.

"I know I don't, but I want to help you out. Anyway, after we've finished, we could go back to mine and spend the afternoon being lazy. If you know what I mean." He grinned wickedly and a dimple appeared in his cheek.

Natalie laughed despite her tiredness and was happy to receive him as he leaned towards her. He brushed her lips lightly with his own, then rubbed her nose with his. His next kiss was hard, and she returned it with equal passion, putting one hand behind his head and running her fingers through his hair. Both his hands held her face before one moved down to cup her breast. He groaned, and she wished she had a place of her own.

CHAPTER 13

The weekend was quiet. Maggie was too tired and wretched to do anything or go anywhere. On Saturday she didn't even get dressed, but rolled around on the sofa, dozed, and flicked through a magazine that Harriet had left on the floor beside where she lay.

Monday morning came and her stomach was still roiling.

"You're not pregnant, are ya?" Harriet roared with laughter when she saw Maggie that morning. "You don't 'alf look pasty." Maggie was tempted to phone into work and tell them she'd had a sick bug all weekend, but Harriet encouraged her to go in. "You'll 'ave to leave this 'ouse and go in to work at some point, so it might as well be today."

Once at her desk, Maggie got on with her work and forgot her worries for an hour or so. It wasn't until her supervisor saw her and remarked on her colour that it came flooding back.

"Are you pining for this bloke?" he asked. "Probably as well you're not with him now. It sounds awful, what happened. I gather the police are thinking suicide. It was in the paper again. Sounds dodgy to me, though. Same thing and same spot as his parents. I mean, what are the chances?"

Maggie's stomach gave a lurch. She needed to get away, right away, but where? Scotland was far away, but maybe that was a bit too different. They had their own laws for some things, didn't they? She didn't even know. She could go to London. Loads of people disappeared there. She couldn't sleep rough, though. And it was dangerous, wasn't it? So huge, too. Perhaps she would simply get on a train and get off at some random place. Somewhere big enough for her not to stand out as a stranger or be recognised, but not too big. Her surname, May, would be a blessing and not easily traceable.

The more she thought about the idea, the better it seemed. Maybe one of those New Towns would be good. She was sure she'd read an article some months ago about one of those. Peterborough! That was where it was. It came flooding back. Several head offices were moving there. They were even giving housing priority to some of the workers. She could go and find a job, surely, if it was a growing place, and she could lose herself in a city like that. It looked nice in the pictures, with a cathedral and everything. Loads of new houses and opportunity.

The grain of an idea planted itself in her head, and before going to catch the bus back to Harriet's she walked to the station. It was a small one but was on the mainline from Southampton to London. She scouted around the ticket office. There were a lot of leaflets in a plastic rack on the wall, but it all looked unhelpful.

"Can I 'elp you, love?" the man in the ticket office said.

"Oh, er, right. I'm wondering about how much it would cost to get to Peterborough."

"Return, that would be?"

"Um, no. Single. Off-peak. Whatever is cheapest."

The man took down a well-used and dog-eared tome from the shelf above the counter. Licking his thumb and forefinger, he flicked the pages. "Yes, 'ere we are. You'd have to change in London and go from Waterloo across to King's Cross. Then you can go straight from there either on a direct train or the slow train, which is cheaper but stops several times. It goes on to York or Edinburgh."

A single ticket would cost a quarter of one week's money. Maggie thanked the man in the uniform and headed home.

As she rode the bus the next morning, she had plenty to think about. Perhaps it would be alright to hang around here. There was nothing to connect her to anyone dodgy, and she didn't know for a fact that Billy had done anything. It was such a coincidence, though, and Harriet had said she'd told him about the visit she'd had from Jay when he'd as good as threatened her.

CHAPTER 14

The last bit of tidying at Moondreams House hadn't taken long. Natalie now lay in Stephen's arms in his bed, after a very satisfying liquid lunch, followed by languid lovemaking. Well, it had started that way then gained momentum until Natalie had cried out and Stephen had gasped as they fulfilled their passion at the same moment. Now, one hand stroked her thigh, and he kissed her shoulder.

"Meeting your mum last night made me wonder," he said. "Got me thinking again about what you told me of your birth parents. Have you thought about trying to find out more? I'd be surprised if Marion would be upset at the thought."

"No, I'm sure she wouldn't. You could see, I take it, from last night, that things are not perfect between Marion and I. Better than they were, but I left hers to live with Dad when I was in my teens. I couldn't take all the lovey stuff she and Dennis showed each other when I was that age. It was all too embarrassing."

"I know. I'm sure she would want the best for you now, though." He continued to stroke her hair and wound a tendril absentmindedly around his finger before freeing it. He then traced a line down her cheek and between her naked breasts, leaning in to kiss her mouth. "It sounds like there was no dad on the scene when you were born, either. So would William mind?"

"I don't believe he would, but I wouldn't know where to start looking for my birth mother."

"If you decide to do it, know that I'd help and support you." Stephen kissed her cheek, and she lifted her face to him.

"It seems such a big thing, and I've thought of little else. I mean, why would she leave me like that? In a doorway, for goodness' sake! I think she must have hated having me. I would have been nothing but a burden, a deadweight pulling her down. I don't think I like her at all, but on the other hand it's like a wound that I can't help probing."

Natalie was surprised to get a phone call from David during her next shift at the bistro. She retrieved her phone from the pocket in her whites and told him she'd ring back at three, as she was in the middle of the lunchtime rush.

She then went onto autopilot while she checked on the tiny cubes of roasted potatoes in the oven and added some herbs before prodding the carrots in the steamer. She pictured the elderly, old-fashioned man, probably in a dark, wood-panelled study at Moondreams House. He would have on his brown brogues, good trousers, his jacket, shirt, and tie, even though he was only at home. He would be sitting at the huge, heavy oak desk with a blotter in front of him, and he was probably using an ancient black Bakelite telephone. Natalie grinned at the thought.

She called him back, as promised.

"The thing is, I was wondering if you would come and meet me at some point soon," David said. "There's a proposition I should like to discuss with you."

"Er … right. Are you able to tell me what it might be about?"

"It's linked to the wonderful meal you prepared for Annie. When might be convenient?"

She agreed to visit him later that week.

As Natalie sat in the taxi to Moondreams House, her mind was buzzing. Both her dad and Stephen were working. She really needed to learn to drive. She had employment at The Wild Thyme Bistro, so she could afford driving lessons now. This made her think of her birth certificate — which she would need to obtain a driving licence — and her mind returned to the mother she didn't know. Did she want to find her?

The taxi pulled up and deposited her in the courtyard, where others normally parked for the dancing class. When Natalie knocked on the kitchen door and peered through the glass, she saw Mrs M waddling towards her to answer.

"Morning, Mrs M," she said. "David is expecting me."

"I'll give him a call. He's expectin' you, you say? You're the lass who was using my kitchen."

"Yes, he is expecting me, and yes, it was me. I hope I left everything as you prefer." Then, she added for good measure, "David was very happy."

"Oh, yes. Righty-o, I'll tell him you're here." She was about to disappear down the corridor when she turned at the door. "Shall I tell him what it's about?"

Nosy old thing, Natalie thought. "He'll know, I'm sure."

As she waited, Natalie looked around. It was a homely kitchen — old-fashioned, but it'd had everything she'd needed.

It wasn't long before she heard footsteps. "Ah, Natalie, my dear. I think we'll go through to my study. Would you prefer tea or coffee? May we have it as soon as you like, Mrs M?"

They went down the corridor and into the hall where the dinner was held. The carpet was back in place, and although the sun revealed the threadbare areas, the obvious quality of it added further refinement to the impressive space. The ancient tiles around the edge looked to be of the period and were probably quite valuable. David led the way across the hall and opened a door to the left of the fireplace.

Natalie could not have been more correct with her imaginings of the study, down to the blotter on the massive old desk. She was offered a seat on one side of the fireplace. Logs were burning, and the tools that lay on the fender matched the brass coal scuttle.

"These old houses are all very well, but the high ceilings and big rooms get cold easily," said David. "Of course, in the height of summer they are cool, too."

Natalie thought he seemed nervous. She was surprised, having assumed he would have the confidence that came with age and experience. However, she also knew that after his wife had died, he'd become almost a total recluse.

There was a knock at the door. "Come!" David leapt up, sprightly despite his years.

It was Mrs M. "Shall I pour?" she asked, probably hoping to find out what was being discussed.

"No, no. We'll manage. Thank you, Mrs M." David watched as she left and ensured the door was closed properly. "Right," he said to Natalie, "you're probably wondering why I have asked you to come. Thank you, by the way."

"It's not far. How may I help you?"

"I've been looking to extend what we do here. The house is Georgian, as I'm sure you are aware. Since Annie brought us her dance school, I've been able to renovate certain areas, as you know. The roof over the ballroom became a necessity, of course."

Natalie nodded and smiled her encouragement.

"It's not the income so much. I can manage what's needed. I was unconvinced at first, and I admit I was reluctant to have people here again. We used to entertain a lot when my wife was here, but over the years, I slipped into enjoying my own company. Probably too much. Now, I think that other people should be able to enjoy the house and grounds. And I have found that I like the company of others again, to my surprise." David stopped and appeared to contemplate his interlinked fingers.

"We're so lucky to be able to use your ballroom," Natalie said, filling the silence.

"Mmm. The thing is… Look, I was wondering about the possibility of having a teashop here. Maybe even serving more substantial food eventually. I know lots of you go to the pub in the village after dancing, but it's a bit … well, a bit of a dive. I did hear rumours of it closing, anyway. I think the landlord's heart isn't in it anymore. I made tentative enquiries about a licence here — I know some people on the council. If we did start a teashop, I wondered if you'd like to run it?"

"Wow! That's a surprise. A teashop." Natalie sat back in her chair, having been perched on the edge. "I know about cooking, of course, but I know nothing much about running a small business."

"I've thought about that too. I haven't said anything to Annie, but I'm sure she would speak to you. She was a complete novice when she started the dance school. A leap in the dark, she said. Her younger brother does all her accounts, I believe. I used to be in antiques back in the day. Of course, I would offer my help and support. We have the space. It needs to be used."

CHAPTER 15

Maggie was sitting on the sofa when the phone rang, and Harriet answered it.

"Maggie, it's for you," she said. "It's the police."

As she rushed into the hall, Maggie shook her head. Her eyes were wide and wild. "I'm not here," she whispered. "Cut the call."

"One moment, please," Harriet said and covered the mouthpiece. "They'll 'ave 'eard you whisper, idiot. It won't be anything to worry about. You 'aven't done anything wrong, 'ave you?"

"No, of course not."

"She's just coming," Harriet said to the person on the line.

Maggie glared at her and took the phone. She listened, her fingers playing with the curly wire. "Yes, of course," she said, "but I don't think I can tell you much. I haven't seen him for several weeks." She listened again and watched Harriet as she did so. She seemed tense as she stood leaning slightly forwards, her hands twisting together. "Yes, that's right. Okay. I'll see you about then. Okay. Thank you. Goodbye." She replaced the receiver in its cradle, ensuring it was the right way round as Jay had trained her to do.

"Well?" Harriet demanded.

"They want to talk to me about Jay."

"About what?" Harriet's voice sounded sharp.

"I don't know. About how he died, I suppose."

"Are they coming 'ere, then?"

"Yes, at about eight o'clock."

"Well, I'll stay clear."

"Don't you do a disappearing act on me," Maggie said.

"Okay, okay, I'll just be upstairs. And don't you be getting in a panic. Remember, you 'aven't done anything wrong. 'E was the wrong 'un in all this. Remember what a bully 'e was and 'ow controlling. Remember 'ow we thought he might 'ave done away with 'is parents. He was a bad 'un and no mistake. 'E got what 'e deserved."

Eight o'clock came and went. Maggie sat on the sofa, clock-watching. Perhaps they weren't coming. Then she leapt out of her seat when the doorbell rang. A uniformed police officer stood on the step. "Miss Maggie May?"

Maggie nodded. Her throat had seized, and her mouth was like sawdust.

"I wondered if I might come in for a moment. I won't keep you long."

Maggie showed him into the sitting room.

The questions were few, and after some minutes Maggie began to relax. Yes, she had once lived with Jay Masters. Mood swings? Yes, definitely. He could be the life and soul, but at other times he was dour and seemed…

"Yes?"

Maggie's mind whirled.

"Other times, you said he seemed … what?"

"Er, depressed, I suppose." Maggie hoped she sounded convincing.

"Depressed, you say? What gave you that impression?"

Maggie knew about depression. She knew about crying for no reason and not caring about what happened to her. Lying in bed with no motivation? Oh, yes. Poor at conversation. Choosing isolation. Oh, yes. She watched the policeman writing that last bit down. Medication? "Sorry, I don't know about that. Like I said, it's quite a while since I've seen him."

"So why did you break up?"

"I couldn't take his moods. Simple as that." She tried to sound relaxed and looked him in the eye.

"Well, thank you, Miss May. I should think that will be all." He rose and made to leave but turned at the door. "Oh, who else lives here? I don't think it's your house, is it?"

Maggie told him and he wrote it down.

As she showed him out, Harriet came down the stairs. There had been no creaking floorboards, no sounds from upstairs at all.

"Did you hear all that?" Maggie asked as Harriet joined her.

"Some of it, not all. It sounded routine."

"Why do they always turn at the door? They all do that on television. They stop on the way out and ask the killer question."

"So, what was the killer one this time?"

"He asked who else lived here." Maggie realised she was going to have to leave.

A week later, Maggie was still feeling queasy in the mornings, and she might even have missed another period. She'd lost track, what with everything going on in her head. Now she was seriously worried. She couldn't bring herself to tell Harriet, and she'd already prevaricated for several days before making an appointment with a doctor she'd never seen before, as a visitor. She chose a practice close to the technical college. Surely they would be more amenable to a young, single woman. Nevertheless, she was extremely nervous and embarrassed. Perhaps that would work in her favour. This was a dreadful mistake. In fact, she could say that if her boyfriend hadn't been killed, they would have married.

The receptionist asked all sorts of questions about where she lived and how long she was staying with a friend. She said she was staying long-term to look after someone who'd had a bad boyfriend experience and was depressed. The woman asked why she couldn't go home to see her own doctor.

"I live up north," Maggie said. "Too far to go, and I don't know when I can get back there."

The woman sighed but gave Maggie an appointment for the next morning. It would mean being late into work, but she could say she had a dentist's appointment.

The doctor was about forty, so that was a bonus. Maggie didn't fancy discussing this with some fusty old codger, nor with someone her own sort of age. He asked if she was on medication, whether she was generally healthy. It was embarrassing when he asked if her breasts had changed. Were they tender or anything like that? He asked about her monthly cycle too, then gave her a small bottle and a funnel and told her to go along the corridor to the toilet.

When she returned, he said, "Well, my dear, I suspect you may be expecting, but telephone my receptionist tomorrow after ten and she'll give you a definite result for this test." He indicated the small bottle into which she had managed to squeeze a little urine. "If you are, you need to make another appointment as soon as possible so we can start the process of monitoring everything and supporting you."

His eyes were kind and, as she nodded to the receptionist on the way out, she wanted to cry.

The next day, the telephone call had to wait until her lunch break, when she could go out to the pay phone down the street. No way did she need this conversation to be interrupted or overheard in the office. The sun was shining and it was getting much warmer, but Maggie barely noticed. Thankfully, no one else was in the box and she pulled open the heavy, red, glass-paned door. She inserted her coins and dialled, taking several deep breaths.

"My name is Miss Maggie May, and I've rung for a test result."

"One moment, please," came the disjointed female voice at the other end of the line. After a pause, the voice asked, "Hello? Miss May, what's your date of birth, please?"

Maggie told her. Her pulse quickened and her breathing rasped.

"Hold the line a moment, please," the voice said.

Oh, why didn't this woman get on with it? She'd run out of coins at this rate. She shoved another in the slot as the beeps sounded.

"Hello?" The voice returned.

Maggie needed to sit down, but there was nowhere. She leaned against the glass panes of the phone box.

"Congratulations, Miss May. It's a positive test result. You'll need to make an appointment to see your own doctor as soon as you can. There will be iron tablets and all sorts of care issues to sort out. Are you still there?"

"Oh, er … yes. Thank you." Maggie replaced the receiver with care and turned to put her shoulder to the heavy door. She almost fell out of it as the person waiting pulled on it at the same time. She gulped the fresh air.

How could she tell Harriet this latest piece of news? She couldn't. She must deal with this herself. But she didn't know a single person who had been pregnant, never mind unmarried and in this position. And it was Jay's child, with his awful genes to inherit. What if they turned out to be some dangerous misfit?

CHAPTER 16

When she next saw Stephen, Natalie quickly filled him in about David's proposition.

Stephen made coffee and passed Natalie a packet of biscuits. "A teashop?" he asked, looking startled.

"I know, that's what I thought. It was a complete surprise."

"What about your job at the bistro?"

"I'd have to keep that on for the time being. My initial reaction was, no way — I couldn't possibly run a teashop. Then I began to think. I'd love to give it a go. But it would need marketing. People might not come at all. It would rely on its name. There'd be no passing trade, of course."

"Plenty of tiny garden centres survive on their coffee shop. People will travel for homemade cakes and a decent coffee. You could do light lunches, too."

"I don't know how I'd have the time."

"Maybe the bistro or somewhere similar would let you work part-time."

"I don't know. It's a massive undertaking. I'm not sure I've got the expertise."

"Don't undersell yourself." Stephen leaned across and kissed her cheek. "You could do it, of course. It depends on whether you want to."

Natalie sighed. She had been content with her reasonable job and this decent guy, but suddenly there were all kinds of chasms opening in front of her. She still wanted to know more about her birth mother and why she'd been abandoned. Now this career opportunity seemed really tempting. She had the drive and the work ethic, of that she was certain, but it was all so new. What if she made a mess of it?

"What did your dad say?" Stephen's words interrupted her thoughts.

"He said he'd stand by me. If I wanted to do it, I'd have his backing. I can keep living at his place, for example."

"Well, then…"

"Yes, but I'd need a business loan from the bank or whatever. What if I couldn't pay it back? It would take time for anything to get off the ground, and I wouldn't be earning for a while."

"Perhaps you could entice investors. Have you spoken to David about it? It was his idea, after all, and it's his old house he's trying to regenerate. Or William. Have you asked him? And what about your mother? You said she was quite financially comfortable with Dennis."

"It's all so complicated. I think I should just forget it."

The more she thought about the way her life was changing, over the next couple of days, the more confused Natalie became. She'd been thrown off course by the discovery that she had been abandoned as a baby. She'd always imagined that her birth mother was a tragic figure. Over the years, she'd built up an image of a lovely lady who had been let down in love, through no fault of her own — or perhaps even someone who had died young and alone. She'd known from a young age that she was adopted but had never thought deeply of her place in the setup before.

Now, instead of thinking that her parents, William and Marion, had chosen her because she was remarkable or important, she began to feel inadequate. Her own mother had rejected her, probably despised her, and got rid of her in the easiest way possible. She'd felt in the way with her adoptive mother, too, as she grew more aware. Perhaps her dad, William, had only allowed her to stay her because he had to. He'd always told her he loved her, and she was sure he did in his way, but perhaps it was a lie that he had persuaded himself was true. She was angry with him for not telling her the truth earlier, and for the first time, she felt unable to share her worries with him. Her thoughts grew and enfolded her in a damp, grey cloud.

Gradually, the teashop venture began to feel like a way for her to find her place in the world, and to rebuild her sense of self-worth.

CHAPTER 17

Maggie would need to concoct a story for Harriet. She'd leave on the train and head for Peterborough. Perhaps she'd just go one day and write a letter, but then she could be traced by the postmark. Not if she posted it in London on her way, though. Neither her friend nor any police would find her, surely, not with a surname like May.

What about work? If she simply walked out of this job, she wouldn't get any money or a P45, so how would she get a job elsewhere? Paperwork was so complicated. It wouldn't be hard to find something if she was prepared to take anything. She might not get office work, but she could work in a shop. If she wore loose clothing, she'd be able to work right up until the baby was due. She'd worry about what would happen afterwards when the time came. Anything might turn up. It was months away.

"How have you been today? Feeling better?" Harriet asked that evening. "Glass of wine?"

"I'll pass on that, thanks. Yes, much better, but don't want to tempt fate." Maggie turned away and found a glass for water. "I ... er ... thought I might go to London for a few days. I've an ancient aunt who hasn't been well, apparently. I might go up at the weekend and see her for a couple of days." Where had that come from? She was getting good at lying.

"Oh? I thought you didn't have any relatives at all. Where did she spring from?" Harriet was frowning as Maggie turned back.

"She's a great-aunt … on my father's side. I haven't seen her for years and years. I just thought it was time. I wrote to her a couple of weeks ago." This was getting complicated.

"Okay. When will you be back?"

Maggie hesitated. "Sunday, probably, but if we get on alright, I might stay until Monday." She thought in haste. If she wrote a letter to Harriet and posted it in London, it wouldn't get here until Monday at the earliest. If she didn't reappear on Sunday, her friend might start a search party and she'd have less time to get away.

"I'm going up for a … um … a lie down. I'll probably come and grab some cornflakes or something light later." She made her escape.

That Friday, having phoned in sick, Maggie left Harriet's house for the last time and walked to the station. She'd need to start thinking more frugally than she had done hitherto. Why was she thinking train when a bus would be so much cheaper? She decided to get a train to London and then go to Victoria bus station to see what was available.

The journey to London was uneventful. The train wasn't busy on a Friday morning. Her thoughts continued to race. She'd need to find a job and soon. Shop work seemed the most likely. Maggie had packed what she could carry and wore her coat with her jacket underneath in case she needed to look smart for an interview. Hopefully, that would be unnecessary for the sort of work she was aiming for. Anonymous work in a small shop somewhere, or maybe as a chambermaid in a hotel. It wouldn't pay much.

The train rattled along through small towns, under bridges and past fields of cows, but the journey was over quickly. Now Maggie had to get from Waterloo to Victoria. It was all so scary. As she exited the station with all its dust and noise and vast empty space above, she shrank against a wall and wondered what to do and where to go. Everyone else seemed to know what they were about, striding ahead on their own or chatting and laughing with friends.

Right, get a grip, girl, thought Maggie. She picked up her bags and found someone in a uniform who looked as if they would know what she should do to get to Victoria.

"Quickest way is the underground, lovey," he said.

"Can I walk?" Maggie asked.

"It's a couple of miles. Takes about three quarters of an hour. Your best bet is Westminster Bridge and past the 'Ouses of Parliament, Big Ben an' all. Victoria Street. Ask again when you get there."

She thanked him. On passing a bank of post boxes, she slipped the letter she had prepared for Harriet through the mouth of the one declaring first class post.

By the time she was walking past Grosvenor Gardens, her arms were aching from the weight of her bag. She saw a policeman and thought about asking him for directions but decided against it. Foolish, probably, she thought, but no point drawing attention to herself. She was determined to hide, to be unidentifiable, unacknowledged. It had all gone wrong with Jay. She had asked for that, she thought. It was all her fault and now she must manage on her own, again.

Perhaps when she had the baby, she would have someone to love and who would love her. Unless the child turned out psychologically dangerous. The thought was a serpent sliding around in her brain. How she would manage, she had no idea.

CHAPTER 18

The days ground on. Natalie slowly began to think she must prove to herself and others that she could do something of her own. She would not be a reflection of her heritage. Nurture not nature. Surely, she had more about her than a mother who'd dumped her and walked away.

Her restlessness came to a head one evening as she sat on Stephen's sofa and sipped her coffee as he read a magazine. When they had made love, Natalie had had a few moments of distraction and had tried to respond, but it hadn't been the best this time.

Stephen sighed and tossed the magazine down beside him. "What's up?" he asked.

"Nothing."

"Is it something I've done?"

"No, of course not. It's not always about you." She was being spiky, and it was unjust. "Sorry. No. It's really not you. I seem to have a lot going on at the moment. That's all. I shouldn't take it out on you."

"Do you want to talk about it?" He was always so supportive, interested and … well, kind.

A guilty spasm rose in her chest. Music played in the background, but Natalie was hardly aware of what it was. Something calm. But all was far from still in her head. Thoughts swirled. A vice of pent-up anger and hurt gripped her chest with jaws of steel. Her pulse quickened. Heat rose up through her body. "I need the loo," she said to Stephen, and she ran to the cool of the bathroom.

As she closed the door, she leaned against it and tried to control her breathing. She was no failure, no write-off, no dead loss. How could Stephen possibly understand? He hadn't been left as an infant. Natalie would be better than her mother who had abandoned her, who didn't care.

She would do something and make a glowing success of it. Perhaps this business opportunity at Moondreams House had come at the precise moment she needed it. She would make it a triumph. It might be tough, but she would overcome any problems.

Then she would find this woman who had left her and rub her face in it. She would show her that she, Natalie, had made a success of her life.

A few days later, Natalie went to tell David what she had decided. He came down to the kitchen, as before, and led her to his study and away from the prying ears of Mrs M. As they went, Natalie remembered what Annie had said about her fear of this man when she'd first met him. He had been gruff and ungiving. He wasn't like that now, but Natalie's heart was pounding anyway.

"So," he started after they were seated, "have you come to some conclusions?"

"I've considered what you suggested, with care," Natalie answered. "I've done some basic work on a business plan. It's something we studied as part of my college course. However, there are some clarifications I would need." She retrieved a folder from the bag she had placed next to her chair.

"It's good to be formal, but also to talk as friends," David said, taking some of the wind from her sails and with it, the confidence she was desperately summoning.

Nevertheless, she brought up her points, one at a time. Which part of the house to use was crucial; the kitchen arrangements and working around Mrs M would be interesting; there were staffing considerations, and she'd need to work part-time elsewhere initially; the list went on. The last point was perhaps the most important.

"I need to discuss the finances. I've looked at what's available on the internet, and there's quite a bit of useful information. I probably need to visit the bank, but I think I also need to encourage investors."

"You're asking me?"

"Er … yes, I am, but then we need to discuss repayment, dividends, or whatever." Natalie knew she was floundering. "I need to do this and make it a success. For me. On my own."

"No man is an island, my dear, to quote John Donne. I know this better than anyone. You may have heard that after my wife died, I shut myself off. Annie and her dance school have changed all that and I owe her so much. This might be my 'pay it forward' moment." David cleared his throat and looked embarrassed at his revelation. "Have you spoken to your father?" he added.

"I've told him what I am considering and where. He's supportive of the idea. He's not in a position to invest financially. There are complicated reasons not to ask my mother and stepfather."

"Mmm, I understand," David said, and Natalie thought he probably did. "Some of it, anyway," he added. "I have a son, but we are estranged. He works in finance but is away in France. So, you see, I do have an idea."

Natalie was surprised but then no one at the dance school knew of her relationships and her birth situation, other than Stephen and Annie.

David continued, "I could invest, rather than you going to the bank. If I put money in, I want to be a sleeping partner, I think the term is. I don't want anything significant to do with the food side of things, serving or being involved with customers. I was hoping you would take over all the food hygiene requirements. I would be happy to invest and be a licence holder, but only for limited hours and provision if we're talking alcohol. I don't want to run a pub here. That is an open book for problems. If I were to invest, we would meet to discuss your plans. Perhaps I would make suggestions because this is my house, but I want it to be a success and I know you have the expertise with food. Perhaps I might bring the experience of organising and running a business from my former years." This was a long speech for David and as they spoke, Natalie warmed to him. To her he seemed a typical elderly gentleman with his round-toed shoes and conventional attire, but he had a kind manner.

"Didn't you say you were in antiques before you retired?" she asked.

"That's right. I started out apprenticed to an auction house, in Bath. It doesn't exist now, sadly. Then I worked at one in London. I worked for myself for quite a while after that."

"Wow. Is that where the lovely things in this house came from?" Natalie looked around at the walls, and then her eyes moved to the huge old desk.

"Some, but I inherited a lot. My grandfather was well-read and well-travelled, and he had an exceptional memory. He often found things while he was away. Some he sold and some are here. He became quite the aficionado of certain Asian pottery, and he bought this house with the proceeds. Anyway, to get back, I might be of some help, perhaps, in decision-making in the early days of our little venture."

"If you are investing, then yes — but, as I said, I do need to do this for me and have the final say in things." Natalie was determined this should be her enterprise, but she didn't want to appear rude, so she added, "We should have a formal document of agreement where your investment is safe for your future. I wouldn't be comfortable taking your money without safeguards. I'd like to reassure you that I can think strategically and without emotion when needed."

"I don't doubt it. I've become adept, over the years, at reading people. It went with my territory. Fear not, my dear, I wouldn't be giving my money away without due thought and proper planning."

"I thought I could run an online thing, too," Natalie said, "selling cakes or afternoon teas delivered to peoples' doors. It would be another outlet and help to spread the word about the teashop here."

"If you are going to work part-time elsewhere while you get this business going, I would be concerned about you taking on too much," David said. "After all, you need to spend time on baking, as well as all the paperwork involved in running a business."

"Yes, you're right. I've considered it, but I need to earn a wage, even if it's not much. I believe I could do it for a short time."

"Have you done a time plan for that?"

"Yes. Here." She passed him a spreadsheet.

"Well, we better go and look at the room I'm suggesting."

Across the hall was a single door that Natalie had never gone through. She followed David across the expanse of old Turkey carpet and experienced a ripple of excitement in her stomach.

She wasn't sure what she had imagined, but the room came as a complete surprise. It had the same huge sash windows as the hall, and it looked as if internal shutters with substantial cast iron ornate handles were folded back into the walls. Floor-to-ceiling curtains in deep red fringed with gold and held with chunky gold tiebacks framed the light that streamed into the room, highlighting the mahogany table that must have been able to seat twenty-two people at least. Currently, the top was covered with a yellow-tinged transparent plastic protector, and a candelabra stood at either end. Mahogany chairs with red velvet padding, which matched the curtains in colour, were arranged under the table. A similar chandelier to that in the hall hung from the centre of the intricate plasterwork of the ceiling and to one side, on the long wall opposite the windows, a similar fireplace to those Natalie had seen elsewhere in the house sat empty. The mantelpiece was rouge marble with fine lines of white and grey. In any other setting it would look over-the-top, Natalie thought, but here it was truly magnificent. The dark, creamy, almost mustard walls were warm, but there was an accent wall against the fireplace covered by lighter paper with a bold pattern. It was all so tasteful and traditional; rich but comfortable.

The only thing that was out of period, although it still looked old, was the floor. Gone were the tiles Natalie had seen in the hall. Here, there was a dark parquet woodblock floor with antique-looking rugs placed in front of the hearth and in the large bay of the windows. "I hope this beautiful floor won't spoil for having tables and chairs and women's heels on it," Natalie said.

"It's deceptive." David grinned. "My wife chose it, but it's some artificial stuff. Looks like the real deal, doesn't it? She was clever and thought of things like that."

In one corner stood a magnificent, lacquered sideboard. David followed Natalie's gaze.

"That's one of the pieces I inherited. I suppose it's quite valuable. I understand it was an altar cabinet from the Shanxi province of China. You can see it's highly decorated, but it's functional. Lots of storage. Probably leave that in here. Useful for cutlery and plates and so forth. The table would go, of course, and I would undertake to furnish the room appropriately. Anything I buy would remain in my possession in case you decide to finish the business in the future. I would consult on what you think we would need, of course."

Natalie was speechless. Eventually she stirred herself. "It's … it's amazing."

"Do you think it would do?" David continued. "The kitchen is only out of the door and down the corridor, of course. Back in the day we had big dinner parties here. We had staff and the food was always hot, so no problem about distance. None of that new-fangled serving hatch business that came in halfway through the last century."

"The only thing I can see as a potential issue for this room is a fire exit. We would need to consult the local fire authority."

"Done. Have a look behind that curtain in the corner. I had to have all that when Annie hired the ballroom, so I had them look in here at the same time."

Behind the curtain was a door which led to the outside of the building.

"You're smiling. Does that mean you think it suitable?"

"Yes," said Natalie firmly.

CHAPTER 19

Maggie got off the coach and looked around. She had arrived in Peterborough. The expanse of tarmac with the coaches and double-decker buses in their bays was daunting. There was the back of a pub on one corner and some small, terraced houses, several painted bright pink or orange, along a road on the other side.

Maggie waited at the side of the coach while the driver came round and lit a cigarette. As it hung from the corner of his mouth, he unloaded all the bags from the cavernous storage compartment underneath. Gradually, everyone reclaimed their luggage and disappeared, some going one way and some another until she was left standing alone and lost. Once more, she was beset with anxious thoughts. Perhaps she should have stayed where she was with Harriet. Then the memory of the visit from the police shot into her mind and cold dread crept down her spine. No, she was better off here — especially with her being pregnant by that animal of a man. How could she have been taken in by him? But she knew the answer to that. She had been taken in by his charming care of her when she was most in need. Then she had allowed him to dominate her life until she had been scared. Really scared.

She moved towards the road where the pub was, and found she was in somewhere called Westgate. She passed an old-looking building with steps and railings up to its door. There was a plaque above the door commemorating, in fancy script, an Edward Wortley Esq., MP for Peterborough. Further on was a smart-looking department store. Mannequins in the windows wore clothes that she had only ever seen her mother's generation wear. It would be okay to work in a place like that, though. She might get a discount on posh makeup. As she walked on, she passed an arcade and finally found a newsagent where she bought a Peterborough newspaper. For once, Maggie had a little luck. She picked the *Peterborough Telegraph*, and it had a houses to let section. However, it was already getting late in the afternoon and Maggie decided she'd better find somewhere to stay for the night.

"Do you know where I might find a cheap hotel or a B and B for the night?" she asked the lady behind the counter, as she handed over her precious coins for the paper.

"Ooh, duck," said the woman. She put her hands into the large front pocket of her overall as she contemplated the request. "It might be best to head for the Town Bridge and go down London Road. There's a few down that way." She gave basic instructions, and with a weary heart and aching arms, Maggie picked up her bags.

She plodded along, barely glancing at the shops she passed. Outside a Woolworths she stopped a young family, who nodded her in the right direction.

There was a bridge that crossed over the River Nene, and the road continued past the football grounds. Maggie stopped to rest again and looked around. Ahead of her and across the road, which was busy at this time of day, she spotted a likely looking guesthouse called The Cedars. It looked like a Victorian building, with bow windows either side of the front door which stood open to the dust. Bits of paper eddied against the walls and the gravel had a profusion of weeds, but she had made it this far without incident, and she couldn't afford to be too fussy.

An hour later, Maggie was sitting in a brown and cream room on a bed with a lumpy mattress. The window was framed with curtains that were slightly too short and looked out onto the pebble-dash wall of the house next door, but it was clean, and she was away from any danger that might result from Jay's death. She had used the toilet down the hall and the bathroom next door to it to wash the dirt of the journey from her hands and face. There wasn't a sound from any of the other rooms, for which she was grateful. She opened the paper she had bought. There was no time to lose. She needed a job and somewhere more permanent to live, ideally within walking distance of the city centre.

As she skimmed down the page of adverts, she found a really cheap room being offered in a house. It was a shared bathroom, of course, but it had its own gas ring and there was a sink as well. She couldn't believe the price being asked. It was vastly cheaper than anything in the North Hampshire area from which she had fled. It was in Woodston, near where she was now, so it wasn't far from the main shopping area and, hopefully, a job.

The price was so good she became anxious about it being snapped up. She decided to go and look at the place — even if it was only from the outside, she could see if it was a possibility.

It stayed light quite late now, and Maggie walked back down Fletton Avenue to the junction with London Road. Following the instructions from the woman at the reception desk, she soon found the turning on her right into Queen's Walk. She'd been told a lot of Italians lived in this area. Most of the houses were tightly packed semis with small frontages. Most had been built around the turn of the century, going by the date plaques on each pair of houses. The first one she saw said 1901, and as she progressed down the street there was 1905 and now 1906. They must all have been built for some purpose. Maybe railway workers. At the library, before she'd left home, she'd read a book that had said Peterborough was a major centre for that in the previous century.

Maggie found the house she was looking for. It had the pretentious name of Northam Villa painted around the small arch of the front door, and a bow window downstairs and a regular one above. Peering down the side of the house she could see that it stretched quite a way, with extensions on the back making it bigger than she'd first thought. As she looked, a light came on in the downstairs window and a woman wearing a flowered overall reached up to draw the curtains.

Summoning her courage, Maggie took the three or four paces to the front door. To her right, on a pane of the bow window was a notice that read: *Room to Let: ring the bell before 7.30 p.m.* She glanced at her watch. It had been a present from Jay in the early days and it was a really good one, so she'd kept it. She'd thought she could always pawn it, if necessary.

Somewhere in the depths of the house, she heard the corresponding jingle as she pressed the doorbell. While she waited for a response, she pulled her fingers through her hair and wished she'd applied some lipstick. Her nerves began to jangle, too. She licked her lips and stood first on one foot and then the other.

A swarthy man answered the door and asked, "Yes? What do you want?"

"I've come about the room."

Maggie jumped as he bellowed over his shoulder, "Isabella! It's for you!" He then turned away without a further word.

Maggie stood awkwardly. The landlady, Isabella, soon appeared and led her to the available room.

"No animals, no children and —" Isabella looked her up and down — "no members of the opposite sex in the rooms." She removed the cigarette from the corner of her drooping mouth. "Any shenanigans like that and you can go up the other end of the road. That's where all that goes on. We're respectable here."

"Of course. I wouldn't dream of that." Maggie was shocked. They stood in a space hardly bigger than a shed. It was shabby in the extreme, but Maggie needed somewhere, and it was in a reasonable location for someone without her own transport. She thought of the little car sitting idle in the street around the corner from Harriet's. She couldn't have brought it. No way could she afford the petrol, never mind all the insurance and everything else that would be due soon.

Maggie looked around and walked across to the two-ring gas burner, which stood on a chipped Formica-topped table. She wiped her finger over its greasy surface. Taking a deep breath, she said, "I'll give you twenty-eight pounds a week. I'm reliable, clean, and quiet. You'll get no trouble from me." She turned away from the woman and fished some money from her bag. "I've got cash, enough for the first month. I'll be working next week, so there'll be no problem for the next few months' money." Maggie couldn't believe she had been so bold. But needs must, and she was learning fast.

Isabella snatched the money from her hand. Licking her index finger and thumb and counting the notes, she secreted them into her overall pocket. The deal was done.

"I'll return with my things tomorrow morning," Maggie said. "Will you be here?"

"I don't live here, but I'll come over at ten. I'll let you in, give you keys."

"Can't I have the key now? I've paid you."

"I don't have it. I'll bring it in the morning, like I said. Don't get your knickers in a twist. It's not me that's unreliable." She sniffed loudly and Maggie was put back in her place.

"Thank you," she said meekly. "Are sheets and pillowcases included?"

"You must be joking. At that price? Sort yourself out. This isn't a hotel, lovey."

CHAPTER 20

William sat opposite Natalie at the little table in the kitchen. A plate of beef stew and vegetables with rich, dark gravy and a mound of creamy mashed potato sat before each of them.

"You're going for it, then?"

"Yes. I am."

"What about funds?"

"Dad." Natalie sighed. "I'm twenty-four. I have to start standing on my own two feet at some point."

"I know, love, but you're still my girl." It was his turn to sigh, but she saw he managed to swallow it. "It's hard after all these years."

"Sorry," she said, and she was. "I've got some savings and … well, David said he'd be a sort of sleeping partner. While it gets off the ground. I shan't need the bank then, and when I want to expand into lunches or whatever, I'll have more of a business background and a fuller plan."

William looked down at his fork, moving his food around. "Why are you really doing this?"

"I've always wanted a café or some place of my own design."

"I suppose so. But Nats, why now, when you've just started such a good job at the bistro? I thought you might work there for two or three years and really build it up, get something behind you and a place of your own again, before moving on."

"I'm not leaving there just yet. It'll take me a while to get this going at Moondreams House. If it's a problem and you want me out…"

"No, no. Never that. I told you before, you have a place here as long as you need, and if you can't pay any rent, that's fine. Absolutely no problem. I mean that." He paused. "You're not going to answer me? Why now?"

A little worm of anger and guilt started to writhe in Natalie's stomach. She couldn't tell her dad about the confusion. It was bound up with him not telling her of her origins until he was forced to do so. Why had he hidden the fact? She was hurt, yet she was frightened of hurting him, too, perhaps because she loved him so deeply. Her thoughts about undertaking this venture to prove to herself and the world that she was not going to be defined by the woman who'd abandoned her also reflected on him. She should be focusing on what she had become because of her dad, yet all she could think about was the mother who she'd never known.

"So, what's next?" he asked.

"I need to ask if I can move about some shifts at the bistro. Maybe drop a couple of the daytime ones. I'm happy to do evenings and I think Rob, who does the alternate ones, would be happy to take more of the daytime work. That way, I wouldn't lose too much income, and I'd have time to do teas and so on at Moondreams. I can bake and freeze cakes. Sandwiches are easy and scones with all the works are a doddle. I told David I might advertise a takeaway service, too. He's going to sort out furniture, and I'll do the necessary for the food hygiene rating. I've got all the qualifications for the preparation and cooking, but the premises will need to be regulated for the food prep areas. I mean, it's all the pipework, paint, and surfaces and so forth. I shall need to talk with David about a staff changing area, but there's the boot room which has a toilet off it. Pest control shouldn't be a problem, but it's something that needs to be verified to get the tick in the box for level-five hygiene. I shall be aiming for top quality. It's out of the way at Moondreams House, so people have to be enticed by its good name."

"You know your stuff. I'm confident of that. You weren't among the top lot in your year for nothing. Just mind you don't overdo it and wear yourself out. And Natalie … don't do this to the exclusion of all else."

"What do you mean?"

"Don't neglect your friends and family. Stephen, for example."

"Dad! Here, this has gone cold." Natalie stood and, avoiding his gaze, took his plate to the microwave. "I'll give it a few seconds' blast. What are you doing tonight?" She congratulated herself for neatly changing the subject.

"Pat and I are going out to the cinema."

"When am I going to meet this Pat? You seem to be seeing quite a bit of each other."

"I suppose we do. It's a good friendship. That's all. You know me. What are you doing? Anything?"

"I'm seeing Stephen. We're going into the city. We'll probably grab a pizza and have a drink, maybe at The College Arms."

CHAPTER 21

Maggie slept like the dead. She shuddered at the analogy. At least she had sorted one of her problems. The biggest one remained. She put her hand on her stomach and realised with a flush that she didn't feel sick. It was such a relief. Perhaps she'd lost it down the loo and never even noticed. Then she grimaced. *Don't be ridiculous*, she thought.

After she had organised herself with keys at her new lodgings and put her meagre possessions away in the wardrobe with the creaky door, she sat on the bed. It was all a bit gloomy. The carpet had shiny round stains on it — goodness knew what they were. The orange and brown curtains hung irregularly on their rod because some of the hooks were missing. The damp patch up in the corner seemed to be getting bigger as she stared and wondered what it was. At least the airer worked, she discovered, when she stood and unfolded it. The rust was starting to show through the paint where successive residents had hung their damp washing. Maggie's knickers were there now. The first thing she'd done was rinse them out so she could wear them the next day. Now she must go out and find some sheets and a job.

She wanted to stay here, curl up on the lumpy bed and weep. It all seemed so huge, so daunting, so impossible. She looked up at the damp patch again and blinked rapidly to stop the tears from falling. Then she took a deep breath, put on her coat and leaving the room, she locked the door with care. She might not have much, but she'd hidden the money, everything from her bank account, under one corner of the carpet. Withdrawing all her money had been the first thing she had done on her way up the main street. She'd have to open a new account at a different branch.

At least the sun was shining. The streets were busy with cars and people. She walked back over the Town Bridge, the way she had arrived. She looked around and saw the name of the street — Bridge Street. She slunk past the police station on the opposite side, quite a large building, crossed a main road and walked past Woolworths. She carried on and walked past an imposing place with a massive set of columns, a coat of arms set in a triangular bit at the top, and steps up to a huge front door. As she gazed at it from across the street, there was nothing to tell her what it was.

Maggie saw a sign advertising Tourist Information. She looked around, but feeling lost among the tall stands full of leaflets, she approached the counter. "Sorry to bother you," she started.

"No bother, that's why we're here," the young woman behind the counter said.

"It's just that I'm new here and I need to find a job."

"Ah well, we don't tell you where they are." She laughed and Maggie shrank inside.

"Oh no, I mean, perhaps you could tell me where the employment exchange is?"

"I think it's the job centre now, but look." She pulled a map of the city centre out. "We're here." She drew a blue cross. "You want to go to here." Another mark on the map. "We've got the cathedral here and shops along here and a theatre, cinema, and library all this way."

Maggie took the paper, thanked the girl, and beat a hasty retreat. She might as well walk and find the job centre, even if it wouldn't be open since it was the weekend. It would give her a chance to explore a bit and a purpose to the day. Looking at the map, she saw a lot of roads with 'Gate' in their name. Westgate, Boongate, Midgate. She passed the cathedral. It looked so peaceful and was right in the city centre. That was a must-see, but not until later.

The building for the job centre was close to the bus station. She was back where she had first arrived. To her surprise, it was open, but she hung back. She'd never been in such a place. It might be full of awful people. Then she mentally shook herself. What a dreadful judgement she had made. She was unemployed and desperate, now.

She marched through the door set in the old stone building. Disorientated, Maggie looked around. There were banks of cards slotted into display frames, and it seemed they were sorted into various types. Maggie headed to one that said 'Retail' and began to scan each card, looking for anything remotely suitable.

She wondered about signing on and claiming benefits, but not for long. She didn't want to be traced. She was scared. What if her details were given to the police? She hadn't been involved in Jay's accident, but she was sure Harriet had had something to do with it. Therefore, she would be under suspicion as an accomplice since it was she who had been his partner, and she couldn't risk it.

She continued to scan the cards and took details of a couple of things that might do. Leaving the job centre, she was hot and sweaty and needed a cup of coffee and somewhere to sit. Weighing up the cost of refreshment against need, she opted for a small, quiet-looking place in the centre, not far from a very gothic-looking building which was a bank. Something else to be explored next week.

Maggie chose a place against one wall. As she hunched over her cup and saucer, she retrieved the notes she had made in the job centre and considered how to approach the information. There was a telephone number and address for each place, but the one that appealed the most invited her to write a letter in the first instance. It offered more money, by far, than the others. On Monday morning, she would dress in her one smartish skirt and a clean blouse, ensure her shoes were dust-free, and head for that department store first.

She thought of the baby that was coming, but quickly shut her mind to that. It was months away, well, at least five months. Plenty of time to work something out.

CHAPTER 22

Natalie had moved fast and done her homework. First, she needed to decide whether to register as a sole trader or a limited company. Fortunately, all the information was available on the internet and David was a great help when they read it together. For some reason, Natalie found this easier than discussing it with her own dad.

Annie arranged a meeting with her younger brother Simon, who would become Natalie's accountant. David did his part, too, and provided chairs and tables with white cloths and glass tops to protect them. They had discussed and agreed what work was necessary, and now they were awaiting someone to come and do some work in the boot room to ensure any prep work in there was compliant. Natalie fully expected to gain her food hygiene certificate for the whole place quite soon.

A name for the teashop was something that she thought about a lot. She had various ideas — The Sweet Sip, Tea for Me, The Tea of Life — but finally came up with Tea and Sweet Dreams, which seemed to fit with the name of the house.

Simon suggested all kinds of savings Natalie could make, from the computer she used, to a room in the house which could be designated as an office. It would all save on tax. Natalie had also asked about Annie's website, and the guy who had done that had agreed to do one for her — he was a friend of Simon's, apparently. It would have a page for takeaway teas as well as photographs of the latest cake creations. She had made one or two suggestions about colours to advance the mood of cosy opulence she wanted to create. Few, if any, local places could boast of being in a stately home environment. She could take on weddings and all sorts in the future. Her ideas were limitless. Now all she had to do was bake and ice some cakes to entice custom. If she built up a stock, she could freeze some and be ahead of herself.

The day Natalie received her five-star certificate for hygiene was one of celebration. There was to be a grand opening, and planning had gone ahead for that, too. It was to coincide with Annie's afternoon and evening dancing classes, and Natalie ensured all was looking good. Beautiful cotton bunting in shades of gold and crimson to match the curtains hung across the wall above the fireplace, and there were two welcome blackboards, one in the hall outside the door and one in the courtyard where people parked to direct them to the front of the house. The heavy entrance door was propped open with a cast iron weight in the shape of a ballroom dancer. David had ordered a ginormous display of red and golden flowers with silvered foliage, which stood on a pedestal in the hall. Flowers were also placed at each end of the mantelpiece, and there was a posy in the centre of each table. All were fresh and cast a delicate perfume across the room. The sun was shining on the bobbing flower heads in the gardens to one side of the long driveway, and it streamed through the tall windows, casting warmth and hopefulness.

A local printer had made leaflets in colours which reflected the brand Natalie was creating, and she had distributed them to most of the houses in the village of Waterthorpe. She had also placed a half-page advert in the door-to-door magazine that was distributed free to all households in the surrounding villages, and posters were placed in strategic positions too.

Everyone who came was to be offered a free pot of tea or a cup of coffee if they bought cake. These were laid out on a wooden counter, and each was under a glass dome. They were extremely enticing, too, according to Annie, Harry, David, and Edith, who had come to look when she'd visited David for morning coffee the day before. There was a chocolate orange cake ten centimetres deep with three layers, orange fondant cream and Terry's chocolate segments all the way round. The coffee and walnut looked a dream, as did the lemon drizzle. For those who didn't want fondant icing, there was a rich fruit cake. Natalie had also made scones to be had with cream and jam and millionaire shortbread with thick, creamy caramel and a good layer of chocolate.

All the cutlery sparkled, and serviettes in a beautiful shade of red complemented the snowy white cloths.

For the official opening, David had organised either prosecco, orange juice or bottled water for people who came. The glasses waited at a small table in the hall just inside the front door, and Ellie, the daughter of Annie's friend, was going to help out for the afternoon.

While she awaited the appointed opening time, Natalie paced. She picked up a knife and polished it again. She smoothed her apron and made certain it was in pristine condition. Finally, the grandfather clock between the windows in the hall struck the hour.

Natalie waited with her smile ready. She paced again. She looked at her watch. She walked to the front door and popped her head out. Her anxiety was palpable.

Ellie had brought her friend, Liv to help. "She doesn't want paying," Ellie whispered. "I persuaded her to come for fun. I thought I could use the moral support."

"You?" Natalie grinned at her. "It's me that needs that."

What if no one came? She would never forgive herself for letting David down, and what about herself? How could she ever get over such a failure?

She was so busy walking to the kitchen and then back again with increasing speed that she missed the sound of a car door, but when she returned to the hall it was only her dad.

"Oh, Dad, it's lovely to see you but…"

Another car door. She looked at William with fretful impatience.

"Take it easy, my love," he said. "Hush now. People never come at the beginning. It'll be alright."

And it was. First a couple from the early class at the dance school arrived and then another two from the later one. Then Christine and her husband James came.

"Oh, Natalie, you clever girl," Christine said as she accepted a glass of prosecco from Ellie before moving into the dining area to take a seat with her husband.

"I'll go and take the orders and brew the tea while you greet people and show them in," Ellie said. Natalie was relieved to have this lass's quiet initiative at her side.

Next a single lady arrived who Natalie didn't know. "Good afternoon," she said. "I decided it was time I was a bit braver, so I've come to investigate."

"It's lovely to see you. I hope this will be the first of many visits," Natalie said.

The lady nodded and smiled and moved into the dining room to sit elegantly at the table in the window, where the sun glinted off her pale hair. She looked out of the window at the garden, and Natalie saw her smile. This was what she wanted for her teashop: relaxation and simple enjoyment of the moment.

It would be so good to get a few more strangers as well as people from the dance classes, she thought. That was where the real potential lay.

Natalie and Ellie were kept busy throughout the afternoon, and they were both pleased that Liv had turned up. Perhaps Natalie could give her a one-off bonus, as a thank you. Natalie had passing words with occupants at each table and smiled until her jaw ached. There was a gentle flow and a quiet buzz of conversation.

"I shall definitely tell my acquaintances, mainly the people I work with," the lady who had sat in the window seat said as she left, and Natalie felt a surge of optimism.

When the first dance class finished and before the second began, there was another wave of guests. These were livelier, as they all knew each other and were exchanging news and impressions of their progress in dancing.

CHAPTER 23

Finding a job was not as straightforward as Maggie had hoped. She wasted no time and on Monday morning, she determined to pound the streets and not just rely on information she had gleaned at the job centre. The burger bar on Midgate had a card in the window, so, plucking up her courage, she went in to enquire. It wasn't busy at that early hour, although some people seemed to want a burger for breakfast. The idea was repulsive to Maggie in her condition. She was surviving on a cup of tea and a piece of bread and margarine.

She spoke to the manager. After a few simple questions, all of which she answered with a mixture of truth and lies, he said, "If you can start tomorrow, the job's yours." The wage wasn't good, and she doubted that amount would be enough to pay for her room. Even with a free meal each night, burger and chips alone would not do. The thought of working with the smell of food frying all day was challenging to say the least. But she couldn't afford to be too fussy. Perhaps she might get a second job somewhere. She wanted the job at the department store, but that wouldn't be settled for a couple of weeks at least, and she needed the money. This was on offer now. Oh, if only she could ask Harriet what she thought. She had no one. Making decisions on her own was so hard.

"Well?" The manager was getting restless and, looking over his shoulder, he shouted at a girl who was talking to another. "Tracey, people are waiting."

The hapless Tracey nodded and turned to get on with her work, but not before she had raised her eyebrows at the manager's back as he turned to face Maggie again.

"Is there training?" Maggie asked.

He nodded. "Not much to learn, but we'll give you someone to follow for a couple of sessions."

"I'll take it," Maggie said. It would keep her going for a week or two. She thought the turnover of staff in a place like this was probably quite high, so if she was lucky enough to get something better, well, she'd just leave. She mentally shrugged but managed a smile. She was becoming a casual, more selfish person, she thought with guilt. At one time, not long ago, she would have been more mindful of the effect of her actions upon others. Now she had to look after herself. No one else was going to do it. The manager, who was no older than she, gave her some paperwork to fill in, but it was minimal. She wiped the crumbs from a table and sat down to write with the biro he lent her.

"Tomorrow at half eight, then," he said. "We'll find you an apron and hat when you come."

That gave Maggie the rest of the day, so she made haste to the department store and rode the escalator to the third floor where the offices were. At the top she dived into the loo, applied fresh lipstick and dragged a comb through her pale curls. Then she joined the short queue to await attention.

She received a set of forms. She glanced around and there was a table next to a sofa, so she asked if she might borrow a pen. The young woman behind the desk smiled and passed one over.

The questions were straightforward, until she needed to add the name and address of a referee. She knew nobody here in Peterborough, and she certainly didn't want to put down her previous employer. She'd just done a runner from there. She didn't want Harriet to know where she was.

Maggie sat back. This was awful. She hadn't thought this through and began to panic. Tears welled and threatened to overflow. She stared at the ceiling, willing them not to fall.

"Are you alright?" a quiet voice at her side whispered before she was aware of the touch on her shoulder. It was the young woman from behind the desk.

"I … oh … I came for this job," Maggie said, showing the title at the top of the form, "but I don't have a referee." She thought quickly. "The thing is, my mother just died, and my father, well, he's not safe to be with. I left home and ended up here. I so desperately need this job." It was all lies again, but she was desperate, and they fell from her lips with ease.

"It's only for a sales assistant," the woman said. "Have you got a landlady or somebody like that?"

Maggie nodded.

The woman sat next to her. "Well, there you go, then. Stick my name down, if you want, for a second one. They aren't likely to ask for that. You're not a mass murderer, are you?" She laughed.

Maggie nearly gasped but was so grateful that she wanted to cry all over again. Instead, she thanked the woman profusely and, having got her name and address, passed her the completed form.

"So, you're Maggie," she said, looking at the papers in her hands. "Maggie, nice to meet you." She sprung up from the seat next to Maggie and beamed down. "Maybe we'll see more of each other if you get this job. I'm Hayley. Good luck. There's no escalator down; you have to use the stairs." Hayley nodded across the floor and tossed her long, dark, permed curls that were so fashionable right now. "See ya," she said and strode back to her desk.

Maggie was absolutely shattered by the end of each week at the burger place. She was unused to being on her feet all day and she detested the way her clothes smelled. All she could do was put them on a hanger by the open window. There was nothing in the post when she checked in her pigeonhole near the front door every morning.

She looked for bar work to supplement her meagre earnings and managed to pick up a position in a pub further out of town. At the moment, she could walk there and back, but she wouldn't fancy that in the winter. It was only for three evenings over the weekends, but it would help. The clientele was better than a city-centre pub where she thought trouble might flare up over nothing, and it tended to be regulars from the local Victorian houses. Many were older men who called in at nine each night for a swift couple of pints and a chinwag before closing time. There were a few younger people early in the evening who had one drink on their way to somewhere else for a Friday evening out. Quite often groups of single lads called in, but any trouble they might cause, they were saving for later on, in the city.

Maggie began to recognise the regulars and was able to remember their drinks and had them under the tap before they could order. They seemed to like that, and she was pleased with herself. It was an old, traditional place with a wooden floor and yellow ceiling from the cigarette smoke that hung there. The customers started to chat and banter with her. It was good to belong somewhere.

And still she waited to hear about the sales assistant job. She was beginning to panic again. She was eating into her savings each week, and that wasn't sustainable. They weren't that great.

Then, one morning, Maggie noticed her jeans were too tight to do up. Her spirits dropped. She could no longer pretend that it would all be fine. Babies needed things like nappies and clothing. She left the top button undone and pulled the zip only halfway, letting her T-shirt hang outside instead of tucking it in. She tied her apron at work loosely so that her profile showed no change, and she made a couple of comments about eating burgers and putting on weight.

Still, she watched the post each day.

CHAPTER 24

Tea and Sweet Dreams had a trickle of people before and after Annie's dance classes and just a few people came in the afternoons.

"Don't worry," William said to Natalie. "It takes time."

"It's alright," David said. "We'll be patient."

"I miss you," Stephen said. "You're so busy. I do understand, honestly, I do, and it will get easier as more people start to realise what a gem you have created. A little more publicity, perhaps."

Natalie was baking again, and Stephen sat in a wheelback chair in the kitchen at Moondreams House as she worked. "What flavour will this one be?"

"Caramel. I'm going to decorate it with tiny squares of millionaire shortbread and let the caramel dribble down the sides of the buttercream frosting. I had thought I'd use Maltesers, but I think millionaire shortbread squares will be more eye-catching."

There was silence for several minutes as Natalie worked and Stephen watched. She loved the cool feel of the fine flour, the delicate scent of the eggs and butter, the rich, throaty aroma of caramel. It was all so soothing. Then Stephen stood and came to her, kissing the side of her neck.

"How much longer? We could grab a beer somewhere when you've finished, or you could come back to my place and we could have one there, and then … well, you know."

"Not sure." Natalie continued working. "I'll get this finished and see what time it is. I think I need to have a meeting with

Simon Holmes." Her mind was still buzzing with ideas. "Perhaps he can reassure me of one or two financial things."

Stephen sighed. "Simon?"

"Annie's brother, the accountant."

"Oh, I remember who he is." A small silence made Natalie glance over and catch his frown.

"It's business."

"Yes, well, do that, if it will help."

Natalie arrived at Simon's house later that afternoon.

"Call me Si, everyone else does," he said. His front door led directly into a tiny sitting room with a table under some stairs at one end. "Take a seat." He indicated a sofa under the front window. "Here, let me take your jacket. Glass of wine or tea?"

"Tea, thank you."

The first time they had met had been at Moondreams House with David. It had been very formal and quite brief. Now it was just the two of them, and Si had suggested meeting at his house because Natalie didn't really want David to hear what she had to say.

When Simon returned from the kitchen, he had two mugs and a packet of custard creams. "Biscuit?" He held out the packet.

Natalie decided she'd risk the embarrassment of crumbs to stop her stomach rumbling. She'd come straight from Moondreams House and had only two or three hours before she had to be at Wild Thyme Bistro.

"So, what's the problem?" Si's grey eyes surveyed her closely.

Natalie noticed that the top two buttons of his shirt were undone, and a smattering of dark hair showed. He had just enough dark shadow on his chin to enhance his jawline, and his wide and generous smile showed his teeth — just one was a bit wonky. It added to the homely kindliness she sensed.

"Not exactly a problem. I'm very grateful to you for donating some time to me."

"That's okay. Annie told me to look after you." He grinned and his eyes lit up. "It's what big sisters do. Boss you around."

Natalie smiled back. "Well, thank you, anyway. The thing is…" She launched into all her misgivings and uncertainties about income versus outgoings.

Simon, in turn, asked her about the prices she charged against the costs of raw materials and numbers of customers. He already had an idea of premises costs from David and had previously told her that they would be negligible in the first two years. After all, David already had to pay upkeep for Moondreams House, and his philosophy was that if he made a little money in the long term, then fine, but he'd rather have people in the house and appreciating it.

Simon was reassuring. "It can take at least two years to begin to make a serious profit with any new enterprise, but you are already covering your costs, which is, frankly, incredible." Then he gave her some practical ideas. "Not really my area of expertise, but what marketing are you planning? I know you put stuff out for the opening, but I mean since then."

Natalie told him about the Facebook page and showed him on her iPad.

"It seems to have everything. Map, contact information, some great photos. Let's just have a look at the page transparency stuff." He clicked here and there. "Looks good to me. What about ads in the local press? The *Peterborough Telegraph* may even print an article if you write something decent and send a couple of good quality photographs. If they have a slow news day, they may be only too pleased to have it.

Then there are all the little village papers. They do adverts and articles, too, some of them. It's a case of word of mouth for a place like yours. There are always these websites like Eat It, and you could introduce a loyalty card. In time, you could do a newsletter linked to your website with a small giveaway for people who sign up, but maybe it's better to wait a few months for that. Then you'll have more information to share."

Natalie and Simon talked more on the subject and her mood began to lighten.

"How about that glass of wine?" Simon said.

Natalie glanced at her watch, hesitated, and then said, "Thank you, Simon. Only a small one, as I have to get to my other job soon. I am a bit more positive now. I'm so grateful."

"Call me Si, remember? Most friends do. Are you always Natalie, or are you sometimes Nats?"

Stephen called her Nats… She shrugged and considered. "Both, I suppose." She realised she hadn't seen Stephen for a while. Time had disappeared so fast. She was so busy.

"Here we go." Si placed two glasses on a small table beside him and poured the pale white wine before passing her one. "Here's to us, Si and Nats, and here's to Tea and Sweet Dreams."

CHAPTER 25

Natalie hadn't worked so hard since her final two terms at college. If she wasn't baking cakes, she was working at the bistro or serving teas and smiling at people while trying to ignore the ache in her back.

The takeaway service had just been launched. Natalie had engaged a young lad with a scooter to deliver for her. He'd seemed reliable when he'd told her his mum had insisted he get some sort of job, since he was leaving school and not intending to go to college just yet. If he still listened to his mum, then hopefully he would be alright for the casual work she was offering. She had considered the takeaway service as a collection-only thing, but as they were a little out of the way at Moondreams House, she judged, there would be more takers if she offered delivery for a small price. Comments from an online survey she had undertaken, backed up this decision. The markup on the teas themselves was healthy and if she could encourage this side of the business, it would also lead to people coming in person.

Three types of crustless sandwiches, a generous-sized scone with jam and a pot of cream, as well as two small cakes and a sachet of good quality tea per person seemed to be going down well. The price was still highly competitive, and this side of things was taking off well. Ellie came in to help her make the sandwiches and she showed her how to lay it all in the specially designed boxes she had had made from a local printer.

The next time Natalie met Si, he was full of praise. Again, he offered her tea or wine, but this time she went straight for a glass of wine. Whether it was because of this or something else she was unsure, but after a second glass she found herself telling him of her need to find her birth mother. After a third glass, she told him how she had been abandoned in a doorway as a baby. That's when tears fell, and he put his arm around her shoulders.

"Here," he said, upon returning from the bathroom. "I don't have tissues, but this is from a new roll." He handed her a bundle of soft paper.

"Thank you." She sniffed and then smiled up at him. "Not very ladylike with red eyes and a runny nose. Not very professional either." She gave a small, self-conscious laugh.

"I hope we're friends now, rather than client and accountant," Si said and touched her arm.

"Yes, thank you. I'm trying to be accomplished but not acting that way, like a mugwump."

"Like a what?" It was Si's turn to laugh. "That's a new one on me."

"Mugwump? It comes from my childhood. It's a Dad word, but I think it comes from America." She giggled. "It's someone who can't, or won't, decide which side they are on."

"I hope you're on my side," Si said quietly. Then he cleared his throat and sat up straighter. "So, what are you going to do? About your birth mother, I mean."

Natalie pretended she hadn't heard the first part. "I think I need to start searching for her."

"Have you discussed it with your dad?"

"Sort of," she said. "He seemed to understand." She paused before continuing. "I'm cross with him for not giving me the whole story when he told me I was adopted. It's driven a bit of a wedge between us. We've always been so close, but now I'm finding it harder to talk so openly with him."

"It might not be easy for him. Perhaps he's worried about what you might discover. Maybe he's frightened he'll lose you."

"I don't think it's that." Natalie sounded confident, but she didn't know what to think.

"Presumably, if you were left wherever, your mother didn't want to be found. I'm guessing there was no father on the scene, either. Have you anything to go on?"

"There was a newspaper clipping with the name of the shopkeeper from where I was found. That's about all."

Si poured the last dregs from the bottle into their glasses. "Perhaps that's your starting point. Find him … if he's still alive. Depends what age he was when you were left there."

"Ah, I know that." Natalie dug in her bag. "I scanned the article Dad showed me." As she unfolded the piece of paper, an overwhelming sense of optimism flushed through Natalie. Perhaps that was the wine, too, but Si was so understanding. He was encouraging her when no-one else seemed to appreciate the importance of this for her. "Look." She passed him the copy she'd made.

"This is great," he said. "Mm, he would be in his eighties now. Maybe he's passed away, even."

"Yes, he'd be that sort of age, but the son may be around still."

"Perfect." He winked at her.

A flush of a different kind rose up Natalie's neck. She was sure it appeared on her cheeks, so she busied herself with retrieving the paper and folding it again before leaning down to tuck it back into her bag.

"You can access archives of local papers on the internet. I think you may have to pay a subscription. If you could trace this guy, this A. Adair, he may be able to tell you something. Anything would help as a start."

"I'll do it." Natalie spoke with determination. Then she looked at her watch. "I'd better go."

"You don't drive, do you? I've had too much. I doubt I'd be legal. Not after all that." Si nodded at his glass, now empty.

"No. I'd better get a taxi."

"Or you could stay." He waggled his eyebrows up and down, which gave his remark a comedy of which Natalie was uncertain.

She looked sideways at him. "I don't think I'll be undecided on that one. No mugwump here now. Stephen may have something to say about that."

"Ah, Stephen! Of course," Si said. "Oh, well… I'll phone for a taxi. Sorry. Don't mind me for trying." He grinned.

When the taxi beeped outside, Si retrieved Natalie's jacket from the banister and after he'd held it out for her, and she'd slipped her arms in, she turned to thank him. He bent to kiss her cheek, and she got a whiff of the wine before she was overwhelmed by something that was either herbal and outrageously expensive or perhaps simply Si. Whatever it was, it confused and excited her.

"Goodnight, Nats," he murmured.

She scurried out to the waiting taxi.

William was talking to Annie at the end of the dance class. He had come to collect Natalie because Stephen was working. She was in the teashop, clearing up the last of the cups and plates, but kept glancing through the open door to where they stood. Her dad wore an earnest expression and at one point, Annie touched his arm. It set Natalie's brain whirring as she imagined the conversation. She moved closer to the open doorway to listen.

"I'm not sure what to do for the best," he said.

"Just be there, supportive when she needs. An open ear and be patient." Annie was always warm and wise.

"She seems cross and irritated by me. I've always known that I should have told her before about the abandonment, when we told her she was adopted, but I don't even know why I didn't, now. I was scared, I suppose. It was easier to let her believe her mother was whatever she wanted, and she's built up some image of someone who was heroic in some way."

As Natalie listened, she understood that she had shifted in her affections recently and guilt washed over her.

"We seem to be drifting apart," William said.

"I'm guessing finding her roots is something she needs to do. Now she knows about it, it'll eat away at her for a while."

"Yes, I think that's it."

"Offer her help," Annie said quietly.

Natalie leaned closer to listen.

"Keep her in your loop and talk to her about it. It'll work out between you, I know she loves you." There was a pause and Natalie was about to tiptoe back across the room when Annie continued. "Perhaps she needs to prove herself."

"What do you mean?"

"Maybe she believes that she needs to prove to herself and the world that she is better than her birth circumstances."

William was quiet for a moment and then he said, "She is working in a determinedly demented way. She's driving herself far more than is ultimately good for her." Natalie tiptoed back and picked up the tray full of crockery and passed through the hall to the kitchen to load the dishwasher. Mrs M would empty it in the morning. They had come to an understanding about that. Natalie gave her any leftover cake to take home as a thank-you.

As Natalie straightened up, her dad came in behind her. "Anything I can do?"

She stretched and turned. "No, all's done. Thanks. I'm ready to go now."

It was quiet in the car until they were halfway home. Then William said, "Do you want to find your birth mother? If you do, please know I'll help you. It won't be easy, and there could be difficulties or even heartache if you succeed."

"I have thought about it." Natalie looked out of the window on her own side of the car. "I think I need to."

"Need to?"

She sat in silence, trying to sort out what she meant. Her dad seemed to understand because he said nothing more, waiting for her to organise her thoughts.

They pulled up outside the house, and he switched off the engine but made no move to get out of the car.

Natalie expelled all the pent-up air in her lungs in a long, slow breath. "I think I need to know what sort of a person she was. Who would leave a helpless new-born like that? Actually, Dad…" She turned to face him at last. "Actually, I'm so angry. I want to give her a piece of my mind and tell her what a useless piece she is."

He reached over and took one of her hands in his. "My darling girl. You will always be my darling to me. Know that I love you, and I'm proud of what you have become, despite anything you may discover. Try not to judge too harshly yet. That's not who you are."

Natalie saw his frown. "Oh, Dad…" Tears spilled over then, and his arm came around her shoulder.

"Let's go indoors. There may be some heartbreak ahead, but we'll manage all this." He smoothed her hair away from her face and tucked it behind her ear.

She knew he loved her, but she still wasn't ready to share the full extent of her thoughts about herself. She wasn't sure of them, anyway.

As she followed him up the front path, she wondered about Stephen, too. She wasn't even sure how she felt about him anymore. She was aware she hadn't really discussed finding her parent with him and had shut him out from her deepest thoughts. Was that any basis for a meaningful relationship?

CHAPTER 26

When an official-looking letter in a long, white envelope appeared in Maggie's pigeonhole, she didn't know what to think. She experienced a mixture of anxiety and excitement. The former in case it was from officialdom like police and the latter because she had been awaiting something from the department store.

She carried it up to her room and placed it carefully on the bed. Once it was open, she read it several times, until she could have recited the contents without looking at it. She was invited for an interview. Maggie waved the paper in the air like a flag of victory and let out a little whoop. There was a bang on the flimsy wall from her next-door neighbour, an old bag who was forever heard but never seen.

There was no need to plan what to wear. She had no choice — there was only her grey skirt. Still, she could ensure it was well pressed. She would have to indulge in the safety pin trick to fasten it and wear her orange and green blouse hanging outside to disguise the fact that the button would no longer fasten around her thickening waist. Her hair was not well cut anymore, but she could tie it back with an orange scarf.

The four days' waiting were interminable and when the day of the interview arrived, Maggie was jumpy with impatience. She perched on a chair in a white corridor, almost shaking with nerves. She wanted to get up and pace the floor but remained where she was.

When the door opened and a middle-aged, solid woman in a dark suit called her in, Maggie leapt up, followed her into a small office and sat opposite her, separated by a light oak-coloured desk.

The questions she was asked bore no resemblance to those she had practised; however, the stories about her background were a different matter. She was able to answer honestly about her experience of the office she had worked in, but the story about her recently deceased mother and her need to move to this area tripped out easily enough. After all, her own mother had died, so she knew what that was like, and she looked suitably upset as she spoke about it.

"Thank you Miss … er…" The woman looked down at the papers in front of her. "Miss Brown." She raised one eyebrow.

Okay, so Brown hadn't been a very original name to choose, but because it was so common Maggie was less likely to be traceable by Harriet, or anyone else.

"Well, I have your reference here." The woman picked up an unopened envelope. "Please wait outside for a few minutes while I make my decision."

Maggie started work the following Monday. The woman who had interviewed her was Mrs Fuller. It didn't suit her nature at all. She was mean-spirited and picky. She liked to boost her own ego by criticising her staff. There was another lady in the department who was between Mrs Fuller and Maggie in age, so there was no particular friendship group to be found, but that suited Maggie. She came across the young woman from the office upstairs, Hayley, a couple of days after she'd started. She was in the staff canteen, getting a cup of tea.

"Hi." She beamed as she came across to sit with Maggie. "You got the job, then. No one asked me for a reference. I doubted they would."

"Yes, I started on Monday. Thank you for your help, though."

Hayley shrugged. "Didn't do anything, but you're welcome. How is it? Are you with Mrs Half-Empty?"

Maggie put her head on one side and looked at her new friend. "Oh!" She smiled when she got it. "Mrs Fuller. Yes. She's a bit relentless."

"An old bag, you mean."

Maggie giggled. "Yes."

"Hey, you and me should go out sometime. I could introduce you to some of the other girls. Oh no, look at the time. Must fly or I'll cop for it." Hayley leapt up before Maggie had to think of an excuse. "See ya."

She was gone like a whirlwind. As Maggie returned to her own department, she thought about the offer Hayley had made. She needed to save every penny if she was to have any kind of help when the baby arrived.

The more she considered her predicament, the more she didn't want this child. It was getting in the way of everything. It wasn't her fault it had happened. It was that bloody Jay. Half the time, he had insisted on making love. Huh! That was a joke. Making love. Taking, more like, and it was hardly love at the end. He'd taken what he'd wanted with no consideration of her, no thought and care, no love at all, really. She'd had no chance to ask about his lack of protection. She'd assumed he would be happy if she fell pregnant. The only time she had dared broach the subject with him, he had been coarse and told her to get to a doctor for some pills.

So here she was, with the consequences. On her own. Getting bigger. Trying to work out what to do. Most evenings she sat in her room, on the bed. The book she was reading currently fell to her lap as she stared into nothingness. She wanted to curl up and cry. Loneliness and fear were overwhelming.

As the weeks passed, her shape changed. She wore clothes that were looser and disguised herself as much as possible with big jumpers. She made comments about needing to eat less and find an exercise class.

Then one Saturday in November, Maggie was feeling particularly low and decided she must stir herself. She was pleased to have the day off work, having spent the last five days on her feet. She looked around the shops and gazed in the windows. So many lovely things. As she wandered through the department store, avoiding the area in which she worked with cottons, wool, and rolls of fabric, she had to pass through the part which sold babywear, prams, and all sorts of paraphernalia, all expensive and all beautiful. A young couple were looking at carrycots. The man had his arm around the woman, and she looked ecstatic. Then she put her hands to her stomach, protecting the child that lay within. Another couple were talking to the assistant, who then went away and returned with a huge pile of baby clothes. With heads together, the young couple fingered the items, and the lady behind the counter bent her head to look at the ticket.

In a flash, Maggie turned and took the first thing she saw — a pale yellow blanket. She slipped it under her jumper and pulled her coat across. She continued to wander slowly around the walkways, fingering clothing and looking at price tickets as if she were a serious shopper. Without fuss and speed, she made her way to the exit, where she exhaled and smiled inwardly. She had shown them.

The wind was gusting as she hastened back to her dingy bedsit. The bulge under her jumper was nestled warmly in the blanket. Her child needed this. It was becoming more and more difficult to disguise her bump and Maggie was becoming more scared whenever she thought about it, so she pushed it away. Something would turn up. She'd manage somehow.

CHAPTER 27

Try not to judge too harshly, Natalie's dad had said. How could she not? Whoever the woman was, she had walked away from her own child. Natalie was cross and hurt, and she failed to understand what could have been so terrible to drive her to do such a wicked thing. Surely there were social security benefits even back then, or someone who could have helped in a hospital. But perhaps the woman didn't go to a hospital to have her? This was a new thought for Natalie. Why would someone take that risk?

What was she like, this woman who was her mother? Maybe she had gone on to have other children, a nice home, a husband. Would she have ever told him her secret? Or perhaps she had lived a nomadic life, moving from one job or one set of accommodation to another. Natalie wondered if the woman had any regrets or whether she had simply buried the memories of a bad experience. However it was, Natalie needed to know.

As for her dad, she was trying hard to act like everything was fine, but she couldn't quite let go of all the hurt and anger at not knowing the truth. Perhaps he never would have told her if she hadn't forced the issue. That might have been better, although she was sure to find out in the end. When she needed her birth certificate for a driving lesson, a passport application or even to get a mortgage or something, it would have come to light, surely. How could he ever have expected to keep it from her forever?

All her waking hours were spent working at the bistro or baking, serving teas or putting together the takeaway boxes at the teashop. During all of this, her thoughts were churning. Sorting facts; hiding from facts.

Adding to her turmoil during this time, Natalie knew she was avoiding Stephen. It was all too much. Her commitment to him was wavering with the weight of her confusion, and she didn't fully understand why when he was always supportive, kind, and loving. She should be like that with him. Was she simply too exhausted? She began to dislike herself even more but seemed unable to alter.

The conversation with Si played in her mind over and over. *Find the guy in the article from the newsagent's shop.* It would be a start in what could be a long and complicated search for her birth parents. Perhaps she should grasp the nettle and do something if she was to move on, or it would always be picking away at her.

There were several phone calls before Natalie made time to meet Stephen, and they agreed he would come while she was clearing up at Moondreams House one evening. She was wiping the sink and draining board when the lights of his van roamed around the walls as he arrived in the courtyard.

"I've missed you," he said as she arrived outside.

"I've been snowed under, that's all," she said and then chided herself for sounding trite and grumpy.

He enfolded her in his arms and stroked her hair. She admitted, silently, that she enjoyed the security and comfort.

She disentangled herself. "Can we talk? Perhaps we could go and sit in the van. It's chilly now."

Stephen was silent as they walked across the courtyard and he unlocked the doors. And he was silent as they sat beside each other, waiting for her to speak.

"I'm thinking I can't do this," Natalie said.

"Do what, exactly?" he asked.

"I have such a lot on at the moment and I'm letting you down. I can't give the time that you want. I can't give enough of myself."

"Is this because of Si? Is that it?"

"No!" Natalie was genuinely shocked. She hadn't thought of Si in that way, had she? "No," she said again. "There are things I need to do."

"Tell me, Nats. Let me in. I can help."

She took a deep breath. "I'm going to start looking for my mother. My birth mother, that is."

"Why now, when you are so busy with work and it's taking off so well?"

"That's exactly why I need to do it now," she said, fiddling with her fingers and avoiding his gaze.

"Okay." He was hesitant, clearly not understanding.

Silence again. Natalie stole a glance at him.

"I can help," he repeated.

"I don't need help," she said, knowing she was being horrid, but unable to stop herself.

"Is that it, then? This is the end?"

"Maybe we should ease off for a while. Until I'm making more sense."

In the dark of the courtyard, she couldn't see the hurt in his grey eyes but she could picture the frown that would be creasing his forehead. He didn't deserve her shabbiness. "It's nothing you have or haven't done. It's me." She was increasingly sorry for the way she was behaving but felt incapable of being more for him.

Stephen started the van, negating further discussion, and drove her home to her dad's. "Will you keep in touch?"

She didn't know if he was cross with her. "Yes, I will. I'm so sorry, Stephen." Tears leaked and silently rolled down her face.

As Natalie turned to close the van door, she saw his cheeks were glistening in the lamplight. Perhaps not cross, then.

William was out when she let herself into the house and climbed the stairs. In her room, she dropped her bag and her coat fell from her shoulders. She collapsed onto the bed and curled up around her pillow. When she was all cried out, she went to splash water on her swollen face and tried to think what to do.

She remembered Si had had a suggestion. She texted him:

Hi, are you home?

Yes. Do you want to come round?

No. Wondered where you suggested I look for the news article about my birth circumstances.

Right. Hold on… BritishNewspaperArchive.co.uk. You have to subscribe. About £10. Or if you know which paper already, go straight to them. They may have their own archives. Sure you don't want to come over?

Thanks. And no thanks. Not tonight. X

Now, at last, Natalie had a plan and she wanted to get to it right away. The archives for the local papers online only went back to the turn of the century. She'd have to email them, unless she subscribed to this other site Si had given her. She loaded that page and searched 'Alex and the relevant date'. Perhaps they had basic information before she needed to pay.

Within seconds, an article was flagged. There was a tiny thumbnail of a page from a newspaper and to the left it said: 'Alex, newsagent, finds baby in his doorway'. Underneath that in smaller black print was a short summary of what she had read on the clipping she had discovered in her dad's drawer as well as the date it was published. Then she read the name of the newspaper, and Natalie could hardly believe it.

It was the *Peterborough Telegraph* — a local paper. She had to find this Alex, though he'd be elderly now. Perhaps he might still be around. The shop might still be there, but it could have been converted into anything after all this time. She didn't know what it was called now, or where it was, but it was amazing that she had been brought up in the same region she'd been born in. She was happier about this than she could have imagined.

Natalie took a deep breath and flexed her fingers, stiff with tension. Next, she Googled the newsagent's name on the off chance that he might be on the internet somewhere, but she didn't hold out much hope. No Alex. It was a long shot. Then she thought of Googling newsagents in Peterborough. Yell.com had several, and many had thumbnail images. Some of the shops led straight onto the street with no doorway, so they were no good. Others had wide glass windows and doors receding in a porch. Any of these might be the one. There could have been changes to the windows in the intervening years, but she thought it was unlikely that the doorway would have been altered. Perhaps she could visit some. Surely the local newspaper would have a record of Alex's address.

When William arrived home that evening, he knew instantly that something was wrong. "Oh, love," he said when Natalie told him about Stephen. She didn't mention her research. "I'm not sure what to say. I can see you're upset. You know I'll support you in whatever way is necessary, but I'm also your dad. I want what's right for you. I want you to be sure, that's all."

"I can't do it, Dad. Not at the moment. There's too much happening. I can't cope."

"You're putting yourself under too much pressure. You're exhausted with it all. Stephen will understand. If he's the right one for you, it'll work out in the end."

"I don't know." Tears fell again and Natalie sniffed.

William passed her a piece of kitchen roll. "How was he?"

"Stephen? Upset, too." William's expression was troubled, and Natalie felt guilty about that, too. This man had given her everything, but there was still a small knot of hurt and anger that he hadn't told her the full facts before now.

"Come here." William held out his arms as he used to do when she was little, and Natalie rested her head in the familiar dent below his shoulder. The scent of him transported her back to her youth, and she was comforted just a little.

CHAPTER 28

As the weeks passed, Maggie's pregnancy was becoming more than an inconvenience. Since she still couldn't picture the mass growing inside her as a tiny human, she began to resent and even hate it. If she wasn't pregnant, she would be able to look for a better job. Until she knew what was going to happen, it was hard to plan for anything. A malaise had overcome her, and Maggie found it hard to do anything constructive. She was frightened and yet couldn't believe what was coming, so she pushed it to the back of her mind.

Still, the work she had was better than none, though she couldn't afford to go out like the other young women at work. It was all so cool, living in a city, and Maggie couldn't do any of it. All because of that … that monster, Jay, and what he had done to her. The rent took most of what she had, and she needed to be inventive with food. Occasionally at the pub, someone would say, "Have one yourself, duck." Maggie would put the money in a pot, and sometimes she would use it for chips on the way home, but usually it went towards everyday living. She lurched from imagining all was well and she would cope, somehow, to being intensely angry with both Jay and Harriet for placing her in this position.

Life was flat, without variation or interest. She couldn't really feel the child inside her, although it gave her a kick every now and then to remind her. The first time she was aware of it, she was measuring out cloth from a large bolt that had been a struggle to get down from the shelf. The customer looked at her oddly when she stopped suddenly. "You alright?" she said.

"Er, yes. Sorry. Must be indigestion."

Maggie was getting larger, but not so it showed unduly if she wore her T-shirts and blouses outside her jeans and skirt. She had a long cardigan which hung loosely and served the purpose of disguise.

Then it began to dawn on her that it would be next to impossible to keep the baby a secret after she'd had it. Where would she put it? She'd never be allowed to keep it in her room. Isabella had said at the outset that there were to be no pets and no children, and anyway Maggie needed to work. The child could hardly stay here on its own all day, but she couldn't afford a childminder. It would need nappies and so many other things. The yellow blanket she'd stolen was hidden away somewhere under the bed; she had pushed it deep into the shadows when she'd realised what she had done.

Also, there was nowhere for the child to sleep or be washed. Maggie could hardly take it down the hall to the bathroom. Others would see and hear her. Perhaps she could manage with this tiny sink — but if it made a noise, the old bag in the room next door would love to tell on her. If Maggie registered for any social help, someone from her past might find her. Images of police, social services, old friends and bad people grew in her mind. Panic started to weave its way into each day. It built and grew until each hour of every day was filled with worry about what she would do, how she would manage. Then an idea came to her when she was having a coffee with several of the young women in the cafeteria at work.

"No way," one of them said, and Maggie realised she had no idea what they were discussing.

"Me neither, not yet, anyway. I'm sure I will when the time comes. I need a bloke first." Hayley laughed. "What about you, Maggie?"

"Sorry?"

"Kids," Hayley said. "Look at that woman over there." She nodded at a young woman jiggling a child on her shoulder and trying to drink a cup of coffee at the same time.

Maggie was covered in confusion and blurted, "No! Absolutely not." Then she took a gulp of coffee, burning her mouth in the process.

"Well, you'll have to leave it in a doorway somewhere if you fall, then." The woman who said this laughed loudly, as Harriet used to do, and they all joined in. Maggie laughed the longest.

All through that week, Maggie couldn't shake the stupid conversation from her mind. Surely this child would be better off with someone else. Since she wasn't registered with a doctor or a hospital, she would have it here in her room, she thought, and then perhaps she could leave it somewhere. She wouldn't leave it to die. That would be wicked. She would entrust it to someone who would care. An adoptive family would provide the love and everything else it needed that she was unable to give. It would be so much better off.

Maggie roamed for weeks, deciding what to do and where. The first place she looked was the delivery bay at the back of the store in which she worked, but quickly discounted this as suitable. She would be unable to watch and ensure it was found quickly and anyway, it was too close. Investigators might even interview all the girls at the store. Then she wondered about leaving it at the hospital somewhere. Maybe in the ladies' toilets. They would be inspected regularly. It didn't seem a nice place to consider, and then she'd have to get in and out again without being seen. The reception area through which she would have to pass was always busy, from what she had witnessed on her scouts around the place.

Then she discovered some shops with a telephone box and a bus shelter nearby. Maggie could stand between them to watch the newsagent owner as he arrived to unlock his shop. She visited twice and bought a trashy paper and a packet of Opal Fruits each time to ensure he was okay. He worked alongside a younger man and was chatty. He reminded her of her grandad, or perhaps that was the sweets. Her grandpa had always had a packet for her when they'd visited back in the day. Never would Maggie leave the baby and not know it had been found. But here, the man would come early to open up before it was busy elsewhere. She could leave the child in a bag or something.

Then, particularly early one morning, when Maggie was watching the place, someone else came to the doorway. This was a shock and her heart beat faster. She discovered that the pile of newspapers for the day was left before the newsagent came to open up his shop. Maggie bought a cheap plastic watch from the market, since she'd long ago pawned the expensive one she'd had from Jay, and noted that the white van with the papers arrived at the same time each morning. It was fortunate that she'd found out. She could have left the child before the delivery man arrived, and it would be him who found it. That wouldn't do at all. He could be anyone. She didn't like the look of his woollen hat, greasy-looking jacket and unshaven face with the cigarette that drooped from slack lips. If she could leave her bundle after he had been, between the stacked papers and the wall in the doorway, it would be sheltered from casual prying eyes until the newsagent arrived.

The pain of the birth was almost unbearable. Thank God her nosy neighbour was out at work, because Maggie was unable to stop herself from crying out. Then there was all that mess afterwards and cutting the cord. How she managed that she didn't know, except that she thought if she killed the thing it would save everyone a problem. She didn't care about herself, never mind this mewling thing that was causing her so much grief.

Maggie tried to keep the sink and the two gas rings clean. Bathing a child was almost impossible with the resources she had there. She was shocked when the little thing nearly slipped from her soapy grasp. It would have rolled off the draining board altogether if Maggie hadn't managed to block its fall with her body. She was cross with the mess of cleansing gel on her skirt and swore. It was at that moment of fear for the tiny thing, that she realised a bond was starting to form. Maggie finally understood that this was a child — a baby girl who deserved a better life than she could provide.

Maggie felt she had hit rock-bottom. She had always been vulnerable to the whims of those around her. Even when she'd been a child with a controlling father and a nervous mother, she'd always known she wasn't good enough. Not tall enough, not clever enough, not sporty enough, not fashionable enough at school. She would love to have taken part in the school play, but had ducked out of the auditions at the last minute, thinking someone was bound to be better than her. It would have been great to get on the dancefloor at the disco with others from her class, but her clothes were all wrong. Anything half decent she did have looked rubbish on her skinny frame, and her hair never fell right. It was curly and insisted on waving around her face. It was easier and safer to stay at home in her room and read.

Being let down by Jay had been her final failure. She now thought that she probably hadn't deserved him; that she'd driven him to be like he was. She'd tried too hard to please him. At least this little girl would end up with a proper family and a decent life.

Two nights after the birth, Maggie slid along the side of the road, close to the wall. Her guilt was all-consuming, yet what other choice did she have? She flicked a glance over her shoulder. There was nobody else about. She'd made sure it was unlikely over the last few weeks with her planning and surveying.

However, her resolve was waning with each step. Tears ran down her cheeks again. She was aching to stop and hold the child against the lead weight in her chest. Her sore breasts needed the release. But if she did, she would be undone and unable to go through with it. Two days ago, she wouldn't have had this desperate desire.

Maggie stopped and sagged against the wall. Perhaps she could manage somehow without having to see this done.

But only last night the old bag in the flat next door had banged on the wall. "You got a cat in there? All that bloody whining. The landlady will have you out if you don't get rid. I'll tell her if it keeps on. Shuddup will you?"

'Get rid.' Those two words haunted her. Is that what she was planning to do? It sounded so forlorn and devoid of emotion, yet here she was, in complete turmoil of guilt and desolation. Other people had a better plan. Other people found care and benefits. Then she remembered why she couldn't seek out the same.

Maggie darted another look around before slipping into the doorway of the newsagent. The heavy pile of papers, bound with string, was there before her, as she'd prayed they would be. She gently laid down the stripey bag, taking one last peep at the child. It wouldn't hurt, surely. She pulled the yellow blanket away from the child's face, and she moved under Maggie's resting hand. Her tears started again. She couldn't see the baby's features in the gloom, but the image of eyelashes resting against rounded, soft-skinned cheeks came to her mind, as well as tiny fists with small, dimpled fingers and perfect shell nails. She caught a whiff of the baby smell and her stomach lurched. One of her tears fell onto the yellow blanket. She reassured herself that the bottle she had left in the bag was still there. The last thing she did before retreating to her hiding place was to take a sheet of paper from her pocket and place it next to the sleeping infant.

She shook as she stood in the space between the telephone box and the bus shelter in the damp of the early morning, and her eyes never left the doorway. If anyone else came by, she was ready to leap out and shout.

CHAPTER 29

Waiting for a response from the newspapers was the most difficult thing. Natalie tried not to check her inbox constantly. In the kitchen at the bistro, it was next to impossible because her phone was in a locker in the cloakroom. She nearly burned a sauce when she nipped out. At Tea and Sweet Dreams, she had to discipline herself to smile and appear relaxed in front of customers, but if she was preparing cakes in the kitchen, she had her phone propped up on a shelf in front of her.

When she finally received an email from the newspaper, Natalie couldn't believe her luck. It wasn't huge, but it was a step forward. They wouldn't give her an address. Their protocols wouldn't allow that, but they were prepared to forward her information to the address they had on their books, although they couldn't guarantee it would be successful.

Natalie was desperate to tell someone. William was out, and anyway she wasn't sure she wanted to tell him. Perhaps it would hurt him to know she was pursuing things with vigour, now. And it would be difficult to share her news with Stephen after what had happened…

So, she sent a text to someone else.

Si responded straight away with a call. "We could go on a crawl this evening, if you like." He laughed. "Not a blokey pub crawl, a newsagents crawl."

"Oh, Si, that would be so great, but I have to work. This is when the hours of my job at the bistro are a real pain."

"It could be you are simply working too many hours," he said.

"True. The sooner I can give it up and concentrate on Tea and Sweet Dreams, the better."

"You're getting there. The takeaway is doing well. You just need to up the numbers accessing the café itself."

"Its's a bit chicken and egg. I need to spend more hours on it but I need the income from the bistro, so I can't spend more time at the teashop," Natalie said. "Anyway, thanks for the offer of the crawl."

"Maybe another time. See you soon, I hope."

"Yes," Natalie said and finished the call. She didn't need any more confusion in her life, and certainly not more relationship problems.

The next afternoon, the teashop was comparatively busy, even before the dance class people arrived. A group of older ladies came in with their knitting. They stayed all afternoon and had second cups of tea and pieces of cake.

"You've made it lovely here," one of the knitters said.

"Perfect for us. Not too noisy or wild," another added.

"A godsend if we can come regular, like. The house is too quiet now I'm on my own."

"I tell you what, love, could I have four of those millionaire shortbread things to take away? I've got family coming by tomorrow. I'll be sure to tell them where I got them." The woman laughed and added, "Though it's tempting to tell a white lie and say I made them."

"You can't polish your halo if you do that." Natalie smiled down at her. "I'm pleased you like them."

How lovely that her little enterprise was beginning to facilitate social interaction and friendship as the lonely lady had suggested, Natalie thought. While she was washing cups, making up two assorted cake boxes to send out as well as keeping an eye on a traybake she had prepared earlier, her brain was fizzing. She needed to attract young mums as well as older customers. This room was simply not appealing to the younger generation. It was great for middle-aged people who wanted gentile and old-fashioned elegance, but it wasn't suitable for toddlers. If only there was another room where the décor was modern. She would like to have a shabby chic ambience with baskets of bright coloured bricks, wooden trains and cars and books for little ones. The mix-and-match bone china teacups and plates were popular, and moss-coloured cabinets would be great for storage. Wooden tables with mismatched chairs would be perfect and easily available from second-hand stores. They could be painted white and have flowered cushions. Matching bunting could be hung around the walls. Natalie could picture it all. She needed another room nearby in which to do all this — and David's agreement, of course. Perhaps this was what a bank loan would be for, and she would be able to go with some business plan success now.

In the meantime, she continued to be grateful for the group of ladies who were knitting and nattering for all they were worth. Another lady came in on her own. She looked familiar.

"Hello," Natalie said. "Have you been before? Do take a seat, and I'll be right over with what we have today."

"I came for your opening, but I'm afraid I haven't been since. I had a day off today, and I thought I'd treat myself."

"Well, you're very welcome. It's lovely to see you again. I'll be right back."

She noticed some of the knitters nod at the lone woman and one said, "Afternoon. Lovely place, this."

Natalie served the woman, who was good-looking and quite elegant. She wore tasteful jewellery that went well with her fine woollen jumper. The green of that suited her colouring. Natalie remembered that she'd come in alone the last time. Perhaps she had some friends who were working today but could be encouraged to join her next time.

When she delivered the lady's tea and cake, Natalie said, "You said you have a day off. That's good. Do you work locally?"

"Yes, I work at the Pearl Centre at Lynch Wood Business Park, so not far at all. It's nice to get out and about a bit."

"Enjoy your tea," Natalie said, "and let me know if you need more hot water or any more cake. We do takeaways too. Perhaps I could give you a leaflet to share with your friends or people at work."

The lady smiled politely. "Thank you."

The next time she looked, the Pearl Centre lady had pulled her chair across to sit with the knitting group and was engaged in conversation with one of them. Then she heard them laugh.

Before she left, the lady said, "I haven't enjoyed an afternoon so much in ages. It's lovely to make new friends. Thank you for chatting with me," she said over her shoulder as she left.

"See you next week, I hope," said one of the knitters.

Natalie experienced a flush of satisfaction and … yes, it was pure joy. Something she hadn't experienced for quite a while. She was so gratified to be bringing about new friendships.

It was nearly nine o'clock before Natalie was finished for the day. William had said he would collect her if she rang, and she was thinking of that when the noise of a car broke into her thoughts. She looked out of the window. It wasn't a car but a van she knew well. It was Stephen.

Natalie watched him take a deep breath before opening the van door and heading towards her. He held a folded piece of paper. As she opened the teashop door, he raised both hands as if surrendering.

"I'm not here to pester. It's just that I found something I thought you might be interested in seeing."

She opened the door wider, and he joined her inside.

"Its's cold out there." He turned his collar back down. It was an awkward thing to do with one hand, since the other held the paper, and Natalie would normally have reached up to help him. Now she held back, feeling awkward.

She stood her ground on the far side of the room and said nothing. Her thoughts whirled as she wondered why he was here.

"I rang your dad, and he said you were still here. He said he was going to come and collect you, but I told him I can give you a lift home." Natalie's thoughts must have shown on her face, because Stephen continued, "Just a lift. Nothing more."

"Fine. Thank you," she said in clipped tones. "What did you mean, you found something?"

"I've been looking on the internet. Nothing else to do," he added pointedly.

Natalie sighed. "Look, if you're going…"

"Sorry. Let me start again. I looked at some sites — Yell, 192.com, and so on. Then I went for a drive around." He looked sheepish.

Natalie's heart began to flutter in expectation. She turned and pulled a chair from under the table and plonked down onto it.

"I've found it."

"You've found it?" she whispered.

"I've found an Andrew. In a newsagent's shop."

Natalie gasped, but then her heart sank. "What's this to do with anything, though?" She sprang up and began to pace.

"Wait a minute. The informant's name on the original birth certificate was A. Adair. Same initial? It *must* be linked."

"Hang on, let me finish. I went in and asked the man behind the counter if he owned the shop. He did, so I hesitated because he's far too young to have been the man in the paper, but then I thought it seemed such a coincidence. Anyway, it turns out his dad used to own the shop, but his name is Andrew, too, so still not right. He doesn't work much anymore, at least not in the early mornings. His son does most of it, but Andrew senior's father was … wait for it … Alex. Alex Adair. He would be the right sort of age."

Natalie's hand went to her mouth, and she sat in silence. Tears, never far away these days, filled her eyes and threatened to roll down her cheeks. She blinked and found a tissue up her sleeve with which to blow her nose, managing to catch the tears surreptitiously. "When … when did you do all this?"

"Over the last few days." Stephen passed her the piece of paper and when she unfolded it, there was the address.

"Thank you, Stephen." She reached out to touch his arm with gratitude.

He became brisk. "Are you ready? I'll take you home. Where's your coat?"

On the ride home, neither of them talked much. Stephen cut the goodbyes short, and Natalie stood on the pavement and watched the taillights of his van disappear down the windy street. After they'd disappeared, she hung her head and pulled her coat around her. It was several moments before she heaved a sigh and turned towards the front door of her dad's house.

CHAPTER 30

The local paper was full of it. Maggie had bought a copy but couldn't bear to read it, although it was hard to avoid the publicity. There were posters, sponsored by the *Peterborough Telegraph*, in windows of shops and on billboards, A-frames and lamp posts. The headlines all referred to the hunt for the mother who must need medical help.

Days passed, although Maggie barely noticed. She'd phoned in sick and spent hours curled up in bed, trying to decide what to do before she managed to go back to work. She spent a morning there, by which time she must have looked so pale and ill that her supervisor sent her home again. She lurched from resolving to move elsewhere to wondering how she could bear to leave this area where her child was being cared for. Maybe Harriet could help her out. No. If Harriet had really been involved in Jay's death, then she was the last person to go to.

It was approaching Christmas. Maggie walked to the far end of the city centre and by the time she got there, her legs were wobbling. The council had Christmas lights along the main street. There was a tree decorated with huge red velvet and gold foil bows which stood outside the cathedral. It swayed as the cold wind encircled it. Maggie studiously avoided the street with the newsagents and she turned down Westgate instead, deciding to go around the block in order to avoid it. A few steps back on herself and she was there.

She took a deep breath and pushed the heavy library door. The building was Georgian and the stone flags beneath her feet echoed as she trod, before pushing open the internal door and entering the warmth of the rooms. She stepped through with pretended confidence, her heart thumping all the while. The lady behind the desk looked up and nodded before she returned her attention to the box of books in front of her.

The room with the reference books and newspapers was further in, so Maggie headed that way. At this time of day, the library was quiet. No mums with toddlers, thank goodness. She couldn't have coped with all that family cosiness or merriment. One or two older children from King's School in their maroon and grey uniforms whispered together. One wore the short, black gown of an older pupil and one had a white-edged blazer, denoting some posh achievement or other. They were confident and proud of themselves, something Maggie had never been. She avoided them.

Fortunately, there were no well-meaning busybodies who wanted to ask her questions. She made for the corner where the newspapers were stored, hung over stout wooden bars on the wall. The local paper, the *Peterborough Telegraph*, hung on the middle rail and Maggie lifted it off, before taking it to the chairs by the bow window.

On the front page, there was an article under the headline which gave the basic details. Near the end was a quote from the newsagent and his son:

"I'm so honoured that they've named her Alexandra, after me," Alex said. "Feels like, you know, a connection."

"I'd say she was clearly loved," Mr Adair, son of the owner said. "It was all very tender." Please turn to page 4.

Maggie turned the pages almost reluctantly. This was another knife in her heart. She did love the baby. She gasped at the realisation and tears threatened to cascade again. She sniffed. Perhaps she should reclaim her child. Then she read the next article. The police. No way could she come forward now. She didn't want to be arrested, maybe sent to prison, and be separated from her baby anyway. No, this was all for the best. If only this ache in her chest would go away. Maggie returned to the paper:

POLICE OFFICER SPEAKS

Supt Paul Moore, officer in charge of operational policing is leading the investigation into baby Alexandra's circumstances.

'I got to the station quite early for that day's work, and there was the usual handover, although there isn't generally much happening overnight. This is a quiet town. Then I was told about the baby found abandoned. The previous shift had already made some enquiries but then we had to start talking to more people. Over the last few days, we've interviewed dozens of people; bus and taxi drivers, shopkeepers, pedestrians, although there weren't many about. We think the baby was left at the newsagents in the early morning between the day's papers being left on the doorstep and the owner of the shop arriving to unlock.

'The jewellery shop has a camera but like I said, it's a quiet spot and we don't have much footage to go on here. We've asked for any motorists who might have been passing to come forward. We've scoured the local neighbourhood and asked everywhere, looking for someone who might be a woman who's recently given birth, carrying something big enough to be a baby.

'We had big hopes for the media appeal. One or two people have come forward to tell us they'd seen someone with a baby that evening or the morning in question: we followed up all of those, but they all checked out. Another line of enquiry was to talk to the local medical community who might have been caring for the mother antenatally. We've spoken to midwives and doctors, but again we've drawn a blank.

"We know the baby definitely wasn't born in the maternity unit at the hospital because we've accounted for all the babies born there over the period in question. The umbilical cord was not professionally cut, which suggests she wasn't delivered by a midwife or doctor.

"We've tried everything and found nothing. I've got to remain hopeful, but it's disappointing. It's likely the mother acted alone, and that she was the one who left Alexandra. Surely someone will remember a woman who was pregnant and may wonder where the baby is.

"There's no criminal investigation here. You can't help thinking there's a desperately sad story out there somewhere."

Maggie paused before reading further. Her mind was whirring. *No criminal investigation,* she thought. *Yet he's making a deal of trouble to find me. No criminal investigation, my arse! I'm going to have to get right away.*

The last article was from a nurse at the hospital:

Nurse Amanda Keenan is coordinator of the neonatal unit at the general hospital.

"I heard about Alexandra as soon as I walked through the doors that morning. I met one of the nurses, and she said: 'I hope you've got your lippy with you — there'll be cameras in today.' Then she told me about the baby left in a shop doorway. When I got to the unit, I went straight over to have a look at her.

"She was lying in a cot, unaware of the hubbub about her, just sleeping and contented, and I felt my heart go out. The mother clearly wanted this child found. Someone loved her enough to leave her where she'd be discovered and protected.

"Over the last few days, so many people have cared. Each day complete strangers have sent gifts and messages for the baby. So many people had this urge to give her something — but of course, no one who could be her mother, and that's the one person we would all like to see.

"What I worry about is, how will Alexandra manage as she grows up? Not knowing who her mother is or why she left her is going to be so difficult. There will be a lot of questions, and few answers. Still, maybe the police will find her."

Maggie lowered her head and tears dripped onto the newspaper. How had she come to this?

CHAPTER 31

Natalie exited the bus station and climbed the escalator up to the shopping centre. She walked its length with determination. A sleepless night of tossing and worrying had ensured an early start, so the shops she passed were only just raising their metal folding shutters and grilles. The cleaners were finishing wiping the chrome handrails and collecting their wet floor signs. Natalie usually enjoyed window shopping as she walked through the Queensgate Centre past John Lewis, M&S, and all the other smaller shops, but now she was on a mission. All night she had worried about her relationship with Stephen and had imaginary conversations with Mr Adair.

The wind whipped her hair as she pushed the heavy metal and glass door to the outside and she turned along the street, past the Georgian building of the old library that was now a nightclub and on to the current library, with its lecture theatre above. Next to this was the complex that included the theatre, but Natalie's attention was drawn to the buildings opposite. She rarely came this far away from the city centre, but she had passed this way occasionally, little knowing that her whole life had changed so dramatically in this spot.

There it was, sandwiched between a fast-food takeaway and a small outlet that looked as if it would struggle to make any money. The newsagent frontage was painted brick below the windows, which turned in towards the doorway, set back a metre in its alcove. So, this was where she'd been found in her striped plastic bag, lying in a yellow woollen blanket.

Natalie's limbs weakened and she leaned against a wall behind her. The door itself had a long window with three small advertising stickers on it and a letterbox near the bottom. Along the top of the whole shop was a broad name fascia painted the same cream colour as the brick below. Above were two curtained windows, one wider than the other. The whole place looked well-appointed and clean.

As she regained her breath, Natalie was tempted to turn back into the library and go up the stairs to the coffee shop. Fear nearly overtook her, but she had come this far, so she crossed the road towards her destination.

Without allowing further hesitation, she pushed the door and heard a bell somewhere in the back. She approached the counter. A man, probably some years younger than she, smiled and said, "Hello. Can I help you?"

Natalie took a deep breath. This was the first step in what could be a long journey. "I'm looking for Mr Alex Adair."

"May I ask what it's about?"

He had the natural suspicion of people who lived in a city, Natalie supposed. She hesitated. "The thing is, my name is Natalie … but it used to be Alexandra … apparently."

The man in front of her frowned for a moment and then he looked incredulous. "Alexandra? You used to be Alexandra?" It was his turn to be short of breath. "Legend! Well, in our family you are." Then his natural suspicion took over. "Are you really her? The…"

"The baby in the bag? Yes, I am. I was." She shrugged and tried a reassuring smile.

"Oh my … bloody hell. Sorry. Of all things…"

"How can I get in touch with Mr Adair? I really need to talk to him."

"I'm really sorry, but my grandfather's not with us. Hasn't been for a long time."

Perhaps the anguish she was experiencing showed on Natalie's face.

"Hang on." The young man turned and disappeared through an open door behind him. Then she heard him bellow, "Dad! Come on down here. Someone to see you."

Natalie waited by the overcrowded counter among the racks of chewing gum and rolls of mints on one side and lottery scratchcards on the other. There was heavy clumping of shoes descending a carpet-less stairway. She cleared her throat, brushed her hair from her face and tried to rearrange her expression as she stood up straighter.

A very slim man with thin lips and large ears appeared at the door. He looked solemn and unfriendly but when he stood next to the younger one, who was more animated, Natalie could see a resemblance. Father and son stared at her without a word, and she stood looking back at them. Her tongue refused to move.

"Hello," the older man said eventually, and he smiled. It changed his whole demeanour and straight away he seemed more approachable. "How can I help you?"

"Dad, it's Alexandra." The son jumped in before Natalie could open her mouth to speak.

Andrew Adair's expression mirrored that of his son moments before. "Alexandra? *The* Alexandra?"

"Apparently, yes I am. The baby in the bag, although now I'm known as Natalie."

"You better come through." He lifted the hinge of the counter at the far end and beckoned her to follow him. "I've a sort of sitting room upstairs. It's a bit basic, but there's a kettle." He turned on the bottom step and stared at her. "I can't believe it." Then he mounted the stairs while Natalie followed. As Andrew filled the kettle and spooned coffee granules into two mugs, he kept turning to look at her as if his eyes were deceiving him. "Honestly, I can't believe it," he said again. "I wish my dad could be here right now. He always wondered what happened."

Natalie stood in the middle of the room, holding her bag in both hands in front of her, unsure what to say or do now she was here.

"Here, give me your coat, duck," Andrew said, using the local term of endearment.

He indicated a chair and she sat. He then folded his lanky frame into another, so they were either side of a stone 1930s-style fireplace with an electric fire. It killed the cold, and Natalie was grateful for it as she sat huddled in her ancient armchair, cradling her coffee cup.

"How did you find me, duck?"

"A friend looked at newsagents in the area and has been asking questions to find Alex Adair, because I found an old newspaper clipping with his name."

"That was my dad, but we use my name for the business. I'm Andrew. I was a young man at the time. I worked here then, but in those days he still ran the business. My lad downstairs is A. Adair, too — he's another Andrew. My wife chose his name. Not very imaginative." He gave a throaty chuckle.

"I'm trying to find information about my birth mother."

"My dad found you when he came to unlock. I came in later, but by then the police had been and taken you. We went to see you in the hospital before you were put into foster care. Were you adopted after that?"

"Yes." Natalie told him of her happy childhood with her dad and briefly mentioned that her mum didn't live with them. "I'm sorry your dad is no longer here."

"Well, he's too old to cope well on his own, but he's happy in the home."

"The home?" Natalie raised her voice. "I thought your son meant he had passed away when he said he was no longer here."

Andrew chuckled. "Oh, bless you, duck. We could go and see him. He'll be dead chuffed to meet you, after all this time. I don't think he'll be able to tell you more about your ma, though."

CHAPTER 32

Maggie was showing around Neve, a girl on work experience from one of the local secondary schools.

"Ooh, Miss, I love your suit. You look so smart!" said Neve.

Maggie smiled. "Thank you, Neve." She could hardly believe that five short years ago, she had been at rock bottom with her hair in a mess and the same clothes washed overnight and put back on. She'd only been a few years older than this girl who stood in front of her. "Right," she went on briskly, "perhaps you would tidy the fabric rolls. We were so busy on Saturday that some of them got put back in a hurry and they aren't wrapped properly. I'm not sure the same types are all together."

"Sorry, Miss, not sure what you mean."

In that moment, Maggie was transported back to her first weeks in the department. She still remembered Mrs Fuller — 'the old bag', as she'd called her — who had ruled her working life when she had started here. When she'd retired and Maggie was offered the post, she determined she would supervise with kindness, understanding and support.

"Feel the cloth, look at the weave," she instructed Neve.

This store was still old-fashioned, and Maggie didn't know how it would continue to compete with the Queensgate Shopping Centre. There were one hundred shops, cafes and a John Lewis as the anchor store, which certainly challenged this place along with British Home Stores, Littlewoods, C&A and so many others. The city was an exciting place to be.

So many years were passing. Maggie now rented a tiny house in Orton Goldhay, the second township to be built during Peterborough's expansion. Buses ran regularly along the designated lanes and took her right into town, and there was a little local shop next door to the new primary school. It was all so handy. She never stopped thinking how lucky she was in so many ways.

She also never stopped thinking about her child. When she would have been five years, four months and three days old, Maggie began to stand at the bus stop on her way to work and watch the children going to school. Frequently, on her day off, she would just happen to be walking past the school at home time. Children would be skipping out of the doors at the sides of the building, with paintings waving in the breeze, or they'd be dancing along, holding their mum's hand. She looked at each little girl and wondered. Of course, it was highly unlikely her little one would be one of these. There were many schools in the area and anyway, her child might have been adopted several miles away. Still, she couldn't help but imagine. She hoped, desperately, that the little girl was having a happy life. Surely, she must be better off. Maggie could barely look after herself in those early days after the birth.

Quite often Maggie would retrieve one of the big boxes from under the stairs. Inside was a card for each of her child's birthdays. Each year Maggie checked in the newspaper to see which book was number one in the chart of paperbacks that day in December. The books, each with a message penned inside the front cover, were neatly wrapped and placed with care in an ever-growing pile. In the newspapers, there were remarkable headlines. Maggie avoided the ones with disasters like the kidnapping of Terry Waite or the Zeebrugge ferry capsizing but also in 1987 the channel tunnel excavations began. 1988 saw the birth of a one-pound coin instead of a paper note. In 1989 the Berlin Wall came down and in 1990 Nelson Mandela was freed after twenty-seven years in prison. She would wait until the end of each year to decide which of the major headlines she would fold neatly into an envelope, on which she would write the year before laying it in the Treasure Box for her child. One Christmas she had spent a small fortune on a Steiff teddy bear. Maggie wondered if she would ever be able to give her little one these treasures. She probably wouldn't want to be found, and her new parents certainly wouldn't want that either. So, the years passed.

Maggie avoided the nightclub in the city. She didn't go into pubs. She did visit the library, but not the one in town — too many memories. However, she soon discovered that things could happen in the most surprising places.

She was absentmindedly shopping in the supermarket when a voice cut across her thoughts.

"Sorry, I think you've put this in the wrong trolley." A man of about her age, judging by the grey at his temples, was holding a four pack of tinned tomato soup. "It is my favourite, but you may miss it when you get home, and your husband is wanting his supper." The crinkles at the corners of his twinkling eyes made her smile in return.

Without thinking, she said, "No husband. Sorry, I was miles away. Still, soup's an easy option for me after a long day in the office, and I think it counts as one of your five-a-day."

They laughed together.

"Oh yes, the dreaded five. Where's the office?" he asked.

Maggie realised what she'd said about no husband and shrank inside. His follow-up question seemed non-threatening, however. "I work in the Pearl Centre at Lynch Wood."

"That's a coincidence, I work on the same complex, but I'm with ad marketing just down the road," he said. "Have you worked there long? I'm surprised I haven't seen you coming and going. I'm sure I would have remembered."

She was unsure if there was an implied compliment in this but then again, it might have been that she was unpractised at talking socially to any man, never mind one who was obliquely attractive. He wasn't ragingly good-looking or anything, but there was definitely something about him. Perhaps it was those eyes, or maybe his broad shoulders in the well-cut dark suit. Still, at his age he must have a history, as did she.

Staying on safe ground, Maggie answered, "I went there just after it opened. I was in retail in the city before that, but originally I worked … well, that was too long ago to mention." She buttoned her lips with haste.

"I've only been there a couple of years," he said. "It's great for me, since I live down the Oundle Road in Botolph Green. Really handy."

"That's a lovely little development."

"Yes, and great access to the country park," he added.

This was going nowhere, and Maggie reached out for her tins of soup. "I'm so sorry," she said as she took them. "I was miles away, thinking of the book I was reading last night."

"I read a lot," the man said. "Since I live alone and there's not much on the television, it's a good way to forget work. Look, I know this sounds corny, but we seem to have things in common. Would you join me for a drink, perhaps on neutral territory?" He gave the engaging smile again. "Maybe at the Boathouse?" He named a pub at one end of the rowing lake, not too far away. "My name's Rick, Rick St George, by the way." He stuck out his hand, so she had to take it. "I know, it's a ridiculous name. I've often thought it doesn't sound real."

He had guessed her immediate thought. "Maggie," she said, but omitted her last name.

"So, about a drink?"

"Oh, I…" Maggie shrugged and shook her head, about to refuse his offer.

"Please? You could tell me what you were reading. Clearly it was good, since you were miles away in it just now."

CHAPTER 33

It was several days before Natalie met Mr Alex Adair. She imagined he would look like an older version of Andrew and his grandson, since those two were so alike. On the afternoon of the visit, she was on tenterhooks waiting for Andrew. She had finished her shift at the bistro and stayed up half the previous night baking so that she could be confident all was ready at Tea and Sweet Dreams before she left home.

The ride in Andrew's car on the way to the care home was tense and quiet. He signed her into the visitors' book in the reception area, where the lady behind the desk greeted her with a bright smile.

"Ooh, he isn't half looking forward to meeting you. He's been full of it, telling everyone many times over who you are. You're famous in here."

Natalie gave a weak smile. Her tummy was fluttering as she followed Andrew along a quiet, carpeted hallway with windows onto a garden on one side and beechwood doors, some of which stood open, on the other. It seemed a friendly place to live, and she was pleased Alex Adair had somewhere like this. He deserved to be looked after well.

Andrew turned into a room and said in a loud voice, "Hello, Dad. I've brought her."

Natalie followed and peered at the man seated by the window in a wing-backed chair. He wasn't like she'd imagined, not one bit. He was tubby and small, with a beard and a rug of grey hair spiking out from his head. The word 'avuncular' sprung to her mind, and when he smiled at her and held out both hands, she was immediately comfortable and stretched out her own to greet him. He smelled of lemons and tweed. His jacket, shirt and tie were as smart as could be, and she guessed it was all for her benefit.

"So, you're little Alexandra. Here, Andrew, bring up that chair. Put it there so she's got the light on her face."

Andrew did as he was bid and perched on the edge of the bed while Natalie sat opposite the old man.

"I'm eighty-nine," he said, "nearly ninety, but I remember it like yesterday. It seems just a *foo* days ago." His Norfolk accent came to the fore. "There you were, lying in that pale yellow blanket. I thought you was a kitten or something, just that tiny mewling sound. Well, when I looked inside the bag, you could have knocked me over." Both his gnarled hands came up and landed on his knees with a snap and he chuckled. "Now look at you." He sat back and shook his head.

"Dad, I'll go and see about some tea," Andrew said. "I'll be back in a jiff."

Alone with this man, the questions swirled, but Natalie said, "I'm known as Natalie now. I was adopted by a couple and now I live with William, who's my dad."

"I gather you want to find out who your mum is." Alex nodded. "I don't know as I can help you much. Why do you want to find her, then?"

Natalie took a deep breath. All of a sudden, she felt able to explain to this kindly man, even though she hardly knew him. "I've started my own business. A teashop. It's starting to do well. I believe it's going to thrive, even. I've been so full of anger since I discovered she left me in a doorway. I want to tell her I'm successful despite what she did. Her genes haven't held me back. I'm not going to be like her."

He nodded and said nothing at first, but perhaps behind his pale blue eyes lurked the wisdom of his many years, because he said, "Perhaps she doesn't have these genes of which you speak. Maybe she did what she had to do to protect you, and it was the hardest, bravest thing she ever did, giving her child up."

Andrew reappeared at that moment with a tea tray.

"Any biscuits there, son?" Alex asked. "Can't have a cuppa tea without a biscuit." He winked at Natalie.

Tears had threatened, but now they disappeared and she smiled back at him.

"Now, I can't tell you anything about your mother, my dear, but I know they all tried hard for months to find her. Have you tried that there DNA stuff? There was a programme on the telly about that a *foo* weeks ago. It's amazing what they can tell you, you know. You should try that DNA thing." He took a slurp from his teacup. "She loved you, you know. She did, I tell you."

"Aye, she did," Andrew repeated from his perch back on the edge of the bed.

Natalie looked across at him and then back to Alex as he sat hunched in his chair, dipping his biscuit in his tea. She waited.

"It were such a loving note … in the bag … with you." Alex nodded at his son and then inclined his head towards the beechwood wardrobe that stood on the far side of the room.

Natalie's heart quivered with anticipation. She watched Andrew as he crossed the room and opened the cupboard door. When he straightened up, he had an envelope in one hand and a folded plastic object with orange, red and brown stripes in the other. Natalie looked at it, but Andrew passed her the envelope first. She glanced across at Alex, who nodded at her, and then she opened it with gentle, reverent fingers.

The envelope wasn't old but the paper inside was cheap, lined and frail, torn from a notebook judging by the ragged edge. It was yellow at the edges, and Natalie handled it with the greatest of care.

"It's yours now, lass," Alex said, and his rheumy eyes were moist. "I've only been its temporary keeper. It's yours to have, now."

Natalie read the note:

Please take good care of my child. I've searched and searched for somewhere she might be safe. You remind me of my grandpa, so I think you'll take care of things. She likes to be on your shoulder when she cries. I've left a fresh mix of milk for her. I hope for a better home than I can possibly give. I'm so full of fear and I'm so, so desperately sorry.

Natalie sat without moving until her shoulders shuddered, and she became aware of a wet blob on her hand, and then another. She realised with surprise they were her own tears. She looked up at Alex and saw a rivulet course down his lined, roughened cheek before she reread the note.

In that moment, she stopped hating this woman.

Natalie replaced the piece of paper in its envelope and looked at Andrew, at a complete loss over what to say or do.

"This is for you, too," Andrew said. "We kept it in hope. We don't have the yellow blanket you were wrapped in, I'm afraid."

He reached out and she took the folded plastic bag.

"I can't thank you enough. It sounds trite, but it's true."

Alex struggled to his feet, using the arms of his chair to push himself as upright as he was able. Natalie put both arms out and gave him a hug. The rough tweed of his jacket was comforting under her cheek, and tears seeped onto his lapel.

"Bless you, child," he said as he took both her shoulders to look into her face. Perhaps he was looking for signs of the baby she had been. "Keep in touch, now, lass. We wouldn't want to lose you again."

"I will," she said. She turned to blow him a kiss at the door before following Andrew back the way she had come less than an hour since.

He insisted on taking her all the way home, despite her protestations that she could get a bus if he dropped her off. He refused her offer of a cup of tea when they arrived. "Not this time, duck. You need to speak with your dad. You make sure you let us know how you get on with any search for her, won't you?"

As she stood in the kitchen with William, Natalie said, "I can't imagine what she must have been through, and after you told me I was so angry and bitter." She was trying to explain what had happened that afternoon and what she had learned, but words were not enough. She realised Alex was probably correct. It must have been a desperate thing for the woman to have done, not uncaring and lazy. Then she watched in silence as William read the precious note.

When he had finished, Natalie gripped the chair back with knuckles showing white. A frown flitted across William's face, but when he raised his eyes to hers there was profound sorrow in them. "I think I understand how mixed up you've been, and I take some responsibility for that," he said. "You've been mad at me, and I've been so unhappy watching you. I couldn't think how to help you. I know now, I should have told you many years ago, and I'm so sorry. As for this woman who is your mother … I don't know the reasons, but she must have been desperate, and she sounds, from this message…" His voice broke and he cleared his throat. "She sounds absolutely devastated and overcome with fear and guilt."

"Dad…" Natalie struggled to say what she must. "I need to find her. Do you mind me continuing to do that? Now I know a little more about what she did… I mean, she left me in the doorway of a stranger, but I think I understand now. It's not that she was feckless or ruthless and selfish." She paced and turned, then raised and dropped her arms. "Before, I wanted to make a success of Tea and Sweet Dreams and find her to prove *I* was none of those things, that I hadn't inherited those things from her."

"I don't think she was those things, sweetheart, and you most certainly are not."

"I'd still like to find her. It's a space in my head that's nagging at me. It's constant. You'll always be my dad. You've been Mum to me, too." She smiled mirthlessly.

"Of course. I understand. It won't be easy, love. She didn't want to be found then, and she might not want to now. There might be any number of circumstances why that may be."

"I know. She might have another family who wouldn't want to know about me. She probably won't want her dark past to come to light. I understand. I do. I'll be sensitive if I ever find her."

"In the meantime, you have a business to run." William gave her a look from under his eyebrows and tried to lighten his words. "Maybe you need to tell Stephen about this latest, as well." He nodded at the envelope lying on the table. "After all, it was him that found the newsagent."

CHAPTER 34

Maggie had often walked from her little house, past the woodland at Longthorpe House, down through the village and across to the weir, then under the dual carriage parkway and along the side of the rowing lake. It made a round trip of about four miles, but she had never ventured inside the Boathouse building, even though a cold, refreshing cider might have been attractive on a summer's evening.

The pub had a pleasant view of the river, where swans would gather, and there were willow trees and other wildlife close by. The Boathouse also had a patio area and a large garden with a small play area for children, so it was popular at this time of year.

Now Maggie sat in the carpark in her little old Fiat and watched. The light breeze played among the leaves, but it was still warm even at this time in the early evening. It wasn't too late to drive away. He didn't seem to be here yet, unless he was already inside. Then again, she thought, if she did bump into him another time, it would be exceedingly embarrassing if she ran away now.

A dark blue Mazda pulled in and as Maggie watched, Rick climbed out and gazed at the other cars. Maggie had ducked down, and then thought how foolish she would look if he'd seen her. When she sat up and peeped, he was moving towards the entrance of the building. She looked in her car mirror, checked her lipstick and hair and, before she could have further thoughts, she followed him into the pub.

It was a large open-plan space with modern furniture, as befitted its age. It smelled slightly of chips and steak, but

Maggie had eaten a small meal before she'd left home so her tummy wouldn't rumble. She spotted Rick almost instantly. His tall frame was easily discernible, standing at the bar wearing well-fitting jeans and a very white shirt, open at the neck. Its short sleeves revealed tanned arms with a smattering of dark hair. He smiled when he saw her and she moved across the floor towards him.

She experienced the awkwardness of the unsophisticated. Should she shake hands? That seemed too old-fashioned. Should she raise her cheek for a light kiss? Oh, how ridiculous he would think her. *Let him take the lead*, she decided. He placed his hand gently on her shoulder and the warmth permeated the thin cotton of her pink blouse.

"What can I get you to drink?" he asked and then dropped his hand and placed it in his pocket.

Maggie had planned this part already. "An orange and soda, please."

"Shall we go outside? It's not too busy midweek, is it? It's still a lovely day."

She followed him and they found a table overlooking the water. He sat and looked relaxed, crossing one leg over the other. *Does he do this often?* she wondered.

Then he answered her unspoken question. "I haven't been here before. One of the guys in the office was talking about it a few weeks ago. To be honest, I don't go out that much."

She didn't know whether to believe him.

They made small talk, looked at the swans, and briefly mentioned work, but by unspoken agreement they didn't discuss that much. After the first quarter of an hour, Maggie began to relax. They talked about books they had each read and discovered they both had a catholic taste that ranged between historical dramas to adventure stories. Rick told

Maggie he also loved a good thriller or cop drama. That led to films, but Maggie had seen few and had never been to the Showcase cinema built out of town so many years ago.

They touched on family, but Maggie's response was guarded. She had none. That would preclude further questions. He only had a brother, since his parents had both passed away. He didn't see his sibling much. They had grown apart in the intervening year when the brother had married, had children, and moved up north. It was his mother who had kept them together, he surmised. Two hours, and a second round, for which she insisted on paying, and then a third, disappeared without her realising.

It was growing dark, and Maggie shivered. When she looked at her watch, she was surprised at the time.

They left the pub garden to head for their cars and a separate route home, but before they said their goodbyes, Rick said, "Would you come to the cinema with me? I haven't been for a long time, and I don't know what's showing, but I've enjoyed this evening. We haven't been short of conversation, have we?" He was talking too much, and it occurred to Maggie that he was nervous and postponing this 'goodbye' stage of their meeting.

She looked up at his face in the fading light — his kind green eyes, broad, smiling mouth with even teeth, brown hair swept to one side but inclined to fall forwards. Not handsome, but appealing in a gentle way. She'd been taken in once before by a pair of eyes, but they had been slate-grey. Surely this might be different. In a flash of uncharacteristic decision, she said, "Yes, that would be fun."

"Shall I collect you or meet you there?"

"I'll see you there," she said and wondered if he would be offended.

"Okay," he said easily. "May I have your phone number? I'll text you when I find out what's on, and we can decide together what we'd like to see."

He's got me, she thought, but she gave it to him.

"I don't even know your surname."

Maggie thought back to when she had told people her surname was Brown. It was only in the last couple of years, when all those troubles seemed behind her, that she had gradually changed everything back to May.

"Your name?" Rick gently brought her back to the present.

He'd got her again, yet this time, she didn't feel trapped. "It's May." She watched as he filled it in on his phone.

"Maggie May. Like the song?"

"It's a long story, but all to do with my parents being in France when I was, you know, conceived." She grew hot and confused before rushing on. "Mum became obsessed with Margaret of Anjou and was reading about her when I was born, so I became Marguerite. Maggie."

"Well, I shall nickname you Daisy from now on. Marguerite daisies have a golden heart. May I?" he said and laughed, placing his hands on her shoulders. "I mean, might I?"

Maggie didn't pull away, and after a second Rick bent forwards and kissed her cheek with warm, dry lips. She caught the scent of him, and her stomach swooped. She vaguely remembered that first meeting with Jay. He had been intense all that time ago. So had she. She had needed him as much as he'd appeared to want her. Now, she wanted to take things slowly, very slowly, and Rick seemed in no hurry either.

When Maggie got home, she hung her bag and jacket on the bottom of the stairs. She loved her little house. It wrapped its arms around her and soothed her. The sounds and the scent of it were familiar and comforting. It was hers and she was safe here, despite the bad press that the area got sometimes. With promotions and more responsibility at work, she'd been able to afford it, and prices had risen dramatically since. Now, it was worth four times what she had paid.

She went to the fridge and found the half-empty bottle of white wine. As she sat on her sofa, kicked off her shoes and sipped, Maggie replayed the evening and was forced to admit it had been good. It wasn't even that she was out of practice — she had no experience at all. Since that catastrophe with Jay in her youth, she had deliberately eschewed all opportunities for a relationship.

Her thoughts wandered, as they so often did, to her child. She would be twenty-four by now. There were four treasure boxes under the stairs full of cards and gifts she had bought for each birthday and to which she had added mementos of significance each year. Maggie hoped her girl was happy. It was too risky to imagine anything else. If only she knew for sure that she had a good life, this terrible guilt might ease. Maybe she would be able to finally relax with the life she had and enjoy a relationship herself. As it was, she couldn't let herself be that happy.

CHAPTER 35

Natalie and Annie stood together in the hall at Moondreams House. Annie had recently given birth to her daughter, Evie, but was now back at work.

"What I could do with is another room," said Natalie. "I've such grand plans, and I do believe I could pull off an extension to the business. I could give up my job at the bistro then and pour all my efforts into Tea and Sweet Dreams. It would benefit David and the house, too. I know he plans to develop the gardens. More income wouldn't be such a bad thing for all of us. You might even get more clients for your ballroom and Latin classes."

"It's certainly a plan," Annie said. "The rota system for looking afterEviethat Harry and I have seems to be working well. He adores being with her. What he really likes is when it's just the two of them and he cooks with her. He shows her how he peels the mushrooms and chatters away, although of course she can't understand yet. I could easily run another class after this second beginners' class I'm running now, and that would bring in more custom for you."

"So many dance classes, now. Who'd have thought it?"

"I know and I'm loving it. I'm planning one for under eights on a Saturday morning. It'll be a mixture of rhythm games and steps. I really like bringing people out of their comfort zones and seeing them develop in all sorts of ways, not just with the dance steps. Remember when Christine and James started and how scrappy they were with each other? Now look at them. As for Morag, she's a different woman. I wouldn't be surprised if wedding bells are sounding before too long. She and Mick get on really well, and she's become so much more confident." There was a pause in the conversation. "Have you seen Stephen at all? You were a great dance partnership."

"I haven't seen him properly since last year, when I told him how I got on with Alex and Andrew from the newsagent," Natalie said. "Old Alex suggested a DNA test, but it's not taken in this country enough yet, only in America. Stephen sent me flowers at Christmas, and I rang to thank him. We had a bit of a chat."

Annie wisely said no more on that subject. "So, these plans for extending the teashop…"

Natalie told her how she needed a second room, since the idea for a different area specifically for young mums had remained an ambition. "I shared my ideas with Simon, and he was encouraging. He said the financial projections for what I'm already doing are sound, and that now is a good time to grow the business."

"My brother knows his stuff. He's been a really useful sounding board for me with the dance school. Have you spoken to David at all? You never know, he may have a space that neither of us has thought about. This house is a rabbit warren, after all."

"Yes, I should. After all, he's approachable enough."

Annie laughed. "He is now. He's a different person from when I first met him. I'll never forget that time when Harry pushed me forward, so to speak, and I had to ask him if I could use his ballroom for eMotion School of Dance."

Natalie went to the kitchen where Mrs M was making hot drinks for herself, Harry, and David. When she asked where they were, the housekeeper said, "They've been outside down by the lake since first thing, but they'll be on their way back up now, so I put the kettle on ready."

Sure enough, they appeared at the back door. "Hello," Harry said. "Ooh, ready for that tea, Mrs M. Any of those choccy biscuits left?"

"I wondered if I could have a word," Natalie said, looking at David, "but if you're in the middle of something, it can wait."

"No, we're done for now."

They took their mugs and Natalie followed David to his study. "I don't think Mrs M needs to be in on the conversation." He grinned as he placed his mug on the little table beside his usual seat and indicated for Natalie to sit opposite. "How are we doing? It always seems busy these days. When we met last month, the figures you showed me are really most acceptable." He still spoke in his old-fashioned way, and she smiled.

"Okay. Here goes." Natalie launched into her idea of another room more specifically for young parents and their offspring. She described her plans for a children's activity corner, more modern décor, and a coffee machine that would sell all the types that younger people expected. She would also continue to offer all the sweet treats for which she was becoming known, as well as some light lunch items.

"What does Simon think? We need to set up a meeting with him and look at spending and projected income."

"In principle, he's positive. The stumbling block would be a space which I could take over."

"Mmm." David steepled his fingers. "What sort of size? About the same as the room you're currently using, I imagine, if not a little larger with all this talk of an activity area for children and so forth. There's the old box room, I suppose, but it needs a lot of work."

"The old box room?" Natalie was puzzled. "It needs to be quite near the kitchen."

"Well, it's along the service hallway from the kitchen but in the opposite direction, towards the back stairs. Haven't you ever seen it?"

"No."

"You must have realised there's a room through there. The outside dimensions wouldn't match up, otherwise. I better show you, but be ready for a shock."

Natalie grimaced and her enthusiasm waned, but she picked up her mug and prepared to follow David across the central hall and down the corridor towards the kitchen. Passing that, he continued down the other half of the dark, narrow hallway and halted outside a door. Natalie judged that this must be on the far side of the kitchen and on the north corner, as the dining room was on the southern one.

"There'll be spiders and all sorts," David said as he turned the handle and pushed the door open with a creak.

After fumbling for a light switch, Natalie could see that the room was about the same size as the dining room. Wooden shutters were closed and so it was dark and musty. A single lightbulb hung bare, but it was suspended on a wire coming from an ornate ceiling rose which matched the one in the other room. The plaster cornice work was as elaborate as that elsewhere in the downstairs rooms of this grand house.

Apart from that, it held little resemblance. There were several ancient leather suitcases of various sizes, two trunks with wooden bindings and sturdy locks, an old lampshade perched on a stack of chairs, and a large, rough, wooden table covered with piles of magazines and papers and many other accoutrements that were barely recognisable. A film of dust hung over everything.

"You understand what I mean about it needing much work, my dear? I seriously doubt it's a possibility."

Natalie shook her head. Then she said with reverence, "It's perfect."

"Really?"

"Yes, absolutely. It's the same distance from the kitchen as the dining room, and away from the rest of the house so you wouldn't be disturbed, and neither would anyone else. The older folk who come now are happy to knit and chatter and relax. Mums with young children can come here to meet each other, knowing their toddlers are happy too. We need to meet with Simon. This is wonderful. Ah! Just one thing." Natalie's enthusiasm took a nosedive. "What about an entrance? We can't have people coming through the kitchen, obviously, and it wouldn't be great to have them coming down that service hallway. It's far too dark and it's a safety hazard, because that's what we use for carrying teas to the dining room. It's a listed building too, isn't it? So, to have a door put on the outside would either be hugely expensive or not even allowed."

"No need. There's a door there already. French doors. Over there, behind that curtain. We could have a proper closer fitted to the top in line with safety regulations and so forth."

Natalie's hopes soared again.

"Are you able to send Simon one of those text things or whatever you do?"

"Yes, I'll do it now." Natalie dug in the back pocket of her jeans and pulled out her phone. He replied straight away, and they set up a meeting for two days' time.

"This new technology is marvellous," David said.

Natalie needed to get back to the subject in hand. She was beside herself with excitement. "How much of that stuff do you need to keep?" She gestured at the pile of debris in the room.

"Probably none," David answered and gave a self-deprecating smile. "I should have got rid of it years ago, but sometimes when you are a little depressed, shall we say, it's difficult to know where to start."

"We might need a skip, then," Natalie said. "I can do a lot of the work myself, and I'm sure I can get people to help." Simon and her dad would join her, she was sure, and Harry might even be persuaded.

When she was on her bus home, David's suggestion returned. She'd got a bit downhearted after meeting Alex Adair, when she discovered how limited and difficult it was to get a DNA sample tested. It was so frustrating. Perhaps it would be best to try the newspaper.

CHAPTER 36

Rick St George was a wonderful companion and one who, in her own view, Maggie most definitely did not deserve. He still called her his 'Daisy May' and they took pleasure in each other's company. They shared the same interests — mainly history and reading. They enjoyed the cinema and walking, and one day when they were strolling through the fields they came across Moondreams House.

"Goodness, this place is different," Maggie said. "I haven't been this way for many years."

"What is it? It looks like some sort of minor stately home."

"It was built in 1800, and I heard there is a ballroom which has a proper dance school these days. It supposed to be magnificent inside."

"Ballet dancing?"

"No, ballroom and Latin. There was an article in the local paper about it a couple of years ago."

"Just before I came to this area, then." Rick took her hand. "Look, there are a couple of noticeboards at the entrance."

"I think this is a footpath that links with the main driveway. I've never been further than a hundred yards beyond the gate. There is a massive double front door with great pilasters on either side. Very grand. I was too scared to go any further."

"Scared?"

"You know me, not the bravest, and it was years ago." She laughed to cover her awkwardness.

"You have too low an opinion of yourself. You're one of the bravest people I know. Look, eMotion School of Dance. Beginners and experienced welcome. Teacher: Annie Moon —

IDTA Fellow," he read. "Sounds very professional. There's a teashop in there, too. Look. Tea and Sweet Dreams."

"Well, it is Moondreams House, so I suppose it's quite an apt name. Shame we're not really dressed for it." She looked down at her muddy boots and scruffy walking clothes.

"You're right. It's somewhere we could visit another time, though, Daisy." He raised her hand and kissed the back as he held it.

Maggie smiled at him.

Later that week, Rick and Maggie sat at the table in the window of the teashop and looked around at the crimson and gold décor and the ornate plasterwork above.

"I do like that moulded panelling. The whole place is grand. It's a treat to come to a place like this." Maggie's line of sight was directed up at the magnificent chandelier.

"Would you like to see the menu?" Natalie asked, appearing at Maggie's side.

"Thank you." She perused the card. "I can't decide. It all looks so good," Maggie said. "This is a lovely gem of a place. I had no idea of the grandeur of it and was only vaguely aware it was here prior to our walk the other day."

"I've been operating for just over a year, although the house is a couple of centuries old, of course. The original owner was into wool production, apparently, but the current owner is gradually renovating the building and developing the grounds on a more commercial basis."

They ordered tea and cakes and Natalie retreated to the kitchen.

"Maybe she needs some help with advertising and marketing," Rick said quietly, leaning forward.

"That's your neck of the woods," Maggie said, "but I think this is somewhat smaller than you deal with."

He grinned. "Just a little."

"How is that deal going with the pet food group?"

"They seemed happy with the portfolio I put together. They want me to rephrase the slogan slightly, but it's only a couple of words. All will be revealed in the fullness of time, I believe."

"Big business, big secrets," Maggie said.

"Yes, but not for long, and that's the only secret I have from you."

Maggie's stomach clenched.

Tea and cake arrived, saving her from responding. "It's lovely to see you both. I don't think you've visited us before." Natalie grinned.

"No, we both took the day off work so we could come. It's a beautiful room, and it's lovely to sit here and look out at the gardens," Rick said.

"It's something the owner would like to develop. He's talking about having the formal gardens revamped, and then there's the parkland for people to come and explore. I'm still growing the teashop, too. I'm working on another room for people with young children. I'm at the decorating stage and trying to decide whether it needs another name and how that would link."

"Exciting times," Maggie said.

"Absolutely. I'm loving it, though. It's a challenge, but there's someone I'd love to share it with, eventually," Natalie said.

"Partner?" Maggie asked, and then glanced at the young woman's left hand.

"No, not that. Right! Is there anything else I can get you? Shout if you'd like more hot water or maybe more cake." She laughed and Maggie decided she liked this lass. She had sparkling eyes and an infectious smile.

"Cake would be lovely, but I better have no more." Maggie mirrored the mirth and patted her stomach. "She seems nice," she said to Rick, after Natalie had left to speak to another customer. She glanced at her watch. "Crikey, look at that. It's so lovely here, the time slips away."

"Relax, Daisy May mine. Day off, remember? Shall I cook dinner tonight? I've a good bottle of red that needs opening."

"We spend so much time together, I don't understand why you won't marry me," Rick said, again. They were sitting in Maggie's kitchen. "We could sell both our houses and buy something together. It makes so much more sense."

"It does make financial sense, but I'm not ready. There are things … things I need to sort out." Maggie turned from him and began to fiddle with cutlery on the draining board.

"Daisy, leave that." He sounded exasperated. "Look at me. You're always prevaricating without explaining why."

"I can't." Maggie covered her face with both hands. If she hid, perhaps it would all go away. Then she clasped her hands and wrung them. "I can't explain. I don't know. I like it the way we are. I do love you, I do, but I can't marry you."

"Anyone would think you're already married or something." Rick's mouth twisted without mirth.

"I'm not. I never have been. That's absolutely not it."

"Then what are you so afraid of?"

"My parents were never truly happily married. There are so many people we each know whose marriages have fallen apart. Why change things when this works so well?"

"Call me old-fashioned." Rick had nothing more to add, apparently, because he took her shoulders. Then, sensing her consent, he enfolded her in strong arms and kissed her hair.

"I do love you," she whispered again, into his shoulder this time, so he took her chin and turned her face to his and kissed her lips. One thing led to another, and they climbed the stairs to her bedroom. He wrapped his arms around her again and with gentle fingers he undid the zip which slid all the way down her back, sending a shiver of desire through her. Her dress dropped to the floor, and she undid the buttons of his shirt before running her hands across his warm skin. They each stepped out of their underwear, in the twilight and shadows. She touched him again, and he laughed softly. That's what she liked about him. Lovemaking, though full of passion, was also filled with ease and joy. She could relax, knowing that whatever they did it was equal, delightful ecstasy for both of them. He lifted her, and she fell with a soft bounce on the bed.

Afterwards, they lay entwined. Rick kissed her hair and stroked her back until finally he unrolled and headed for the shower. Maggie lay watching the stars and listened to the water running. As she so often did, she tried to analyse her reluctance to marry this perfect man, but she had no logical reason. She didn't deserve this happiness, that was all, and false superstition held her back. If she pushed contentment too far, all would crumble and anything she had now would be lost forever. She couldn't do that to Rick, and she didn't want that for herself either. She had to cling to things as they were and not upset any equilibrium.

As he emerged from the bathroom with the light behind him and his skin still damp from the shower, she experienced desire once more.

Much later that evening, after Rick had left, Maggie sat in the armchair with her feet tucked up and a cup of hot chocolate at her side. She picked up the newspaper to look desultorily at the television listings. As she turned the pages, something caught her eye and chilled her blood.

The headline in the personal pages read, *Searching for her Mother*.

CHAPTER 37

The best thing seemed to be the telephone, for speed. Natalie needed to know how much it would cost to place an advertisement in the *Peterborough Telegraph*.

"Dad, where are the Yellow Pages, please?" Natalie called upstairs.

"Probably in the cupboard under the stairs. Don't use it much." He arrived behind her as she scrabbled about in the confined space.

"What do you need it for?"

"I wanted the telephone number for the *Peterborough Telegraph*. I looked online and I could email, but the number wasn't readily available. I thought I might get a phone response more quickly."

William entered the cupboard and there was a crash and a curse. "Got it," he said. "Everything fell off the shelf together, though." He handed her the directory. "I hope it's worth it. I'll just stack those things back and then we could have a cuppa."

"Good idea, and thank you." Natalie kissed his cheek before heading to the kitchen to fill the kettle.

"So, what's this all about?" William nodded at the fat yellow catalogue lying on the table as he handed her a mug.

"I've been thinking about getting a DNA test. All you have to do is send a saliva sample and it can tell you your regions of heritage to quite a fine degree. They also let you know if there are any other people with the same components, or whatever it is."

"Ah, I see."

"It's not readily available in this country," Natalie went on with obvious frustration. "But I could put an advert in the local paper. You know the sort of thing — 'Looking for my mother' or something. Since my story was originally reported in the *Peterborough Telegraph*, it might work."

"Yes, it might. I hope it does." William hesitated.

"I know what you're thinking. She might not see it; she might see it and not want to respond or … well, I thought it was worth a try."

"How does it work? You don't want to put out your contact details for all the weirdos to get in touch."

"Hence Yellow Pages. I'm going to telephone the paper and ask just that."

The wording for the advertisement took Natalie forever to decide. In the end she opted to keep it simple, so the headline was *Searching for her Mother*. The wording of the text was equally simple. She stated her first name and age and said she was looking for the mother with whom she'd lost contact in December 1985. She decided that was enough information, if the woman in question were to see it. However, she also added that everything would remain confidential and that there was absolutely no question of responsibility. That had been the most difficult thing to word. She didn't want to use the word 'blame', nor did she want anyone to think she would be a burden, financially or otherwise.

William looked at the rough copy and said, "You can do no more. I truly hope it gets you somewhere."

The advert was to appear on the right-hand side of the double page and above the fold. Natalie's research had told her this was the most viewed position. It was a little more expensive than elsewhere, but she decided that if she was doing it at all, she might as well do it properly. She could do nothing but wait. The newspaper said they would contact her if there were any responses.

The first call Natalie received relating to all this was unexpected. She was in the new second dining room at Moondreams House, perched precariously on a ladder with a paint roller in one hand and the tray on the flat part of the ladder at the top. She rested the roller in the tray and managed to wriggle her phone out of her back pocket without falling. It was Stephen.

"Hi," he said, "it's me. I saw your advert in the *Peterborough Telegraph*. How are you?"

Natalie's heart gave a little jump, and her breath left her lungs. "Hang on a mo." She sat down hard on a chair in the corner. "Sorry, I was up a ladder. I'm alright. Yes, the ad. It seemed the only thing I could do to move things forward."

"You're clearly still searching, then."

"Yes." This was not going how she had imagined. She wanted to tell him how much she missed him and how sorry she was.

"Have you had any takers?"

"Takers?"

"Has anyone responded?" Did he sound exasperated with her?

"Stephen, can we meet?" Natalie blurted out.

He sighed and there was a long pause.

"If you don't want to…"

"I'm at the hospital. I'm working late, but the day after tomorrow I finish at four."

"I'll be at Moondreams House, but I'll finish at five."

"I'll collect you. See you in a couple of days," he said, and then he was gone.

Natalie continued to sit disconsolately, looking down at her phone. *He didn't sound very enthusiastic*, she thought. *I can't blame him*. She looked around the room, which was gradually coming together. It didn't seem so exciting right now. She wanted to share it with someone. No, not just anyone. She needed to share it with Stephen.

CHAPTER 38

If the advert had upset Maggie's equilibrium, the newspaper article was a hundred times worse.

On her way home from work, she'd bought a copy of the *Peterborough Telegraph* at the newsagent-cum-post office. Settling down in her chair for a relaxing hour before she would prepare a light supper, a huge headline caught her attention. Her veins seemed to hollow, leaving her trembling and cold.

The article had been written by a journalist who was now freelance, apparently, but he had worked on the original case of the baby left in the doorway, he said. Maggie hesitated before reading on, held back by horror but desperate to discover something, anything new. The story recapped everything that had passed all those years ago.

Maggie read through tears that streamed uncontrollably. From the comfort and warmth of her little room, curled up in the armchair as she was now, she saw in her mind the desolate, dank room in which she had been living then. She remembered the awful décor with the ill-fitting curtains and stained carpet, the tiny electric fire which was all she'd had to keep her warm, if she could afford it, and the sorry state of her clothing. The time she'd nearly dropped the baby on the floor because it was so slippery, and she was too inexperienced to know what to do. The author of this piece had no knowledge of her dragging exhaustion and worry, her utter desperation to earn any pittance that she could in order to feed herself.

Then came the plea for new information from the young woman searching for her birth mother. There an air of wretchedness in what she said, as she told how the wondering never left her. She only wanted to find the woman who was her mother, and she would try to understand the agony of the act she had performed in leaving her child.

The young woman explained how she had met up with the newsagent after all these years. At least Maggie had chosen well there, it seemed. The woman was no longer Alexandra, but Natalie, and she stated what a kind and sensible man the newsagent was and how he had cared about what happened to her for all these years. Maggie's sobs increased until she was hiccupping with grief. She had cared for all these years too, but had been unable to discover anything due to her own fear and cowardice. How despicable she was.

It was at that moment that the doorbell rang, and she heard a key in the lock. She gasped and held her breath.

"Hello, Maggie. Sorry, it's only me." Rick's voice rang out. "Maggie, are you there? I think I must have left my phone here."

She heard him go into the kitchen. "Maggie!" he called again.

With that she gave another loud and tearful hiccup, and the door opened as she was scrubbing at her face with a handful of tissues. Rick's head appeared.

"Maggie, my darling, whatever is the matter?" He crossed the floor in two strides and knelt down in front of her with his arms wide. She untucked her legs and pitched forwards into the comfort of his embrace, where her tears continued.

He hushed and rocked as if she were a child, and slowly the waterfall subsided until all that was left was exhaustion, her gasps for breath, his sodden shoulder.

She came to the only decision she could, and turned from him, found the paper that had ended up crumpled behind her, and thrust it at him. He took it and she saw the frown etched on his brow as she watched from the corners of her swollen eyes. He scanned the article. The frown deepened. Maggie knew this was the end. When she told him her connection, he would hate her and all that she had done. Her shoulders slumped. Perhaps it was better. She had managed before on her own; she could do it again.

"I don't understand." Rick's puzzlement was writ large on his face, and then the truth began to dawn. "Do you mean this is you? You left a baby in a doorway?"

Maggie closed her eyes and nodded, before she whispered, "I was desperate. I was totally alone. Someone had to give this poor child a better life than me." Her head hung.

Rick stood and dragged his hands through his hair, blowing out his cheeks. Then he turned and left the room.

Maggie heard him fill the kettle and retrieve mugs from the cupboard. She dithered and didn't know whether to follow him or wait for his return. She took a deep breath and went to stand in the kitchen doorway. The heavy gnawing pain in her chest was almost too much. "I wasn't much more than a child myself. I left the man because he was abusive, and I was truly frightened." She was stricken with shame.

Rick carried on with his task, neither turning nor apparently listening, but Maggie ploughed on.

"Then I heard he was killed … in a road traffic incident. Next thing, I discovered I was expecting his child."

Should she tell him about Harriet and her suspicions? Why not? His opinion must already be at rock-bottom. In the light of all these intervening years, well, she realised she hadn't done anything to cause Jay's demise. She truly was innocent of that. "I moved to Peterborough to get away from the friend I was living with. I didn't trust her anymore. I think she was involved in the man's death. I was so scared."

Rick did turn then. "What? Are you saying it wasn't an accident?"

"I don't know. I simply don't know." Maggie wiped her nose and eyes again.

"And were you involved in his death?" The question was asked quietly.

"No. I wasn't, Rick, and that's the truth, but I was young, alone and very frightened." She told him of Harriet and what she had said about her friend, Billy. "I fled. I came here — well, to the city — and I hid myself. It seemed far enough away. I got a job in a shop, but I couldn't manage, and when the baby came…" She leaned against the door jamb, weak at the knees. She turned away and went back into the sitting room before she collapsed onto the edge of the chair and put her head in her hands.

Rick followed with the mugs of tea, which he placed on the mantelpiece before sitting on the sofa.

Her head still bowed, Maggie said, "Shame and guilt and fear has stopped me becoming close to anyone, ever." She looked up and met his eyes. "Then I met you. I learned to live a little. I learned to love you."

"But your love has always been too civilised, too controlled. This is why, I suppose," Rick said.

An involuntary sniff passed, and Maggie hung her head again, so she didn't hear Rick come and stand before her.

He bent and took her hand. She looked up and he raised her to her feet. He gave a monumental sigh. "Knowing all this … well, I know you as you are now. That's the you that I love. I'm guessing that you thought you had no choice. If you were alone … I don't love you any less, but I need to understand, and it'll take time."

He drew her gently into his embrace.

CHAPTER 39

"I saw the advertisement in the *Peterborough Telegraph*, and then today I saw the article on page three. A half page," Stephen said to Natalie, having picked her up in his van. "*Still Searching for her Mother*. Great article."

"Yes — the newspaper rang again. I was hoping perhaps they'd had a response from my advert, but it was a different department asking for an interview so they could write that article. I was so surprised. They even said they'd do a follow-up with a photograph next week. I'm a bit nervous about it all now."

"Why?"

"It … well … it seems to be having a life of its own. I don't know really," she finished, feeling feeble.

"I'd have thought you'd be pleased. If it helps to find your mother, then it's surely all good."

"My dad is highly supportive, which is amazing of him really. I was mean to him, too, because he hadn't told me anything for all these years." She paused for some minutes and sat in difficult silence. "I'm lonely, Stephen, and a bit scared." She flicked a glance at his profile, lit by amber light as they passed the streetlamps.

He said nothing.

She tried safer ground again. "In the article, I tried to ensure what I said held no accusations of blame. It was a hard interview to give. I wanted to make sure there was enough information, but I didn't want to put her off if she considers getting in touch."

"That would be via the newspaper, would it?"

"Yes."

"I noticed it gave your first name but no personal stuff."

"That's right. They suggested that was safest, to stop cranks from getting in touch."

"Right."

Natalie was aware that Stephen's responses were mainly monosyllabic, and she was awkward too. They rode on in silence for several more minutes, until they turned into the pub carpark. As it was so early, it was almost empty.

Natalie had dragged a brush through her hair before Stephen had collected her and then waited at the door to the courtyard. They hadn't gone into Moondreams House, so she'd had no opportunity to show him her latest project. She'd avoided that subject on this short journey. This meeting wasn't about her — she wanted it to be about Stephen's feelings and making things better.

As they moved towards the pub entrance, Stephen strode with his hands in his pockets. Natalie tried not to blame him for the chilliness between them. She was the one who had stepped back.

He bought the first round and they sat in awkward silence again. Natalie knew it was up to her to start the conversation. She cleared her throat and took a deep breath. "Stephen…" He looked at her, but his eyes gave nothing away. She crashed on without finesse. "Stephen, I'm sorry. I have huge regrets about us becoming so distant."

Again, he said nothing.

"I got myself in a right muddle and made a mess of things." She played with her glass. "When I discovered the circumstances of my birth mother leaving me like that, I was cross with Dad because he didn't tell me before — I know now that he was trying to protect me — and I was furious with

205

her, for doing that to me. Well, the fury was rooted in hurt and upset and not understanding how things might have been for her. I got this warped idea that she had faulty genes and that I had inherited her recklessness. I wasn't thinking deeply enough."

A flicker of puzzlement on Stephen's face creased his brow. "I still don't see what this has to do with me. You cut me out of it all. I tried so hard to help you, and you didn't want to know."

"I know that now." Tears threatened, but she did all in her power to stop them falling. She cleared her throat again and took a gulp of her drink.

"So?"

"I ploughed everything I had into Tea and Sweet Dreams. I had this idea that … that if I could make a success of the business, I could find her and gloat that I wasn't like her. That I wasn't feeble and irresponsible." Her chin sank onto her chest. "I'm ashamed of what I became."

"I see." She heard his intake of breath.

"That's not me. It's not. Maybe it was for a time. I've hurt you and I've realised how important you are to my life. You didn't deserve my treatment of you. I'm so, so sorry." Then, in a small voice, she added, "I miss sharing things with you."

"Me too," Stephen said quietly, and Natalie hardly dared to breathe with the hope his words brought.

"When I met Alex — and that was through you, I know — he helped me to see that my mother must have a been a brave and determined person to do what she did. It would have been one of the most difficult things, surely, for a mother to give up her child. The note she left reflected that. I lost my perspective."

Stephen put his hand out across the table, palm up. Natalie reached for it, and his warm fingers curled around her own and his thumb grazed her knuckles. The tears did fall then. Without relinquishing her hand, he came around to take the seat next to her, and she was aware of his arms around her, hugging her close, shushing and rubbing her back. "Oh, Nats. What a tale it is. Hush now. Whatever happens, we'll see it through together, if that's what you want."

"Oh, it is. It truly is."

"Hush now. I wish you'd told me all this before. I thought you had gone right off me, and the more I thought that the more I tried to help. All these thoughts about genes and…" He kissed her curls. "I even wondered if you and Si were having a fling." He pointed at the apple juice she'd ordered. "Do you really want that?"

She smiled. "No, not really."

He arose without checking. *He knows what I would really like*, Natalie thought, as she watched his adorable backside and broad shoulders retreating. She was proved correct when he returned with a small glass of clear white wine.

"You better tell me what you've been up to at Moondreams House," he said.

After Natalie had described her colour scheme and her ideas behind the second tearoom, he said, "It's not late. How about we go and take a look? You have the keys."

Her spirits lifted. "Really? Now? Are you sure you want to?"

"Nats, calm down. I said, didn't I?" He gave a gentle laugh.

The design of the room was almost the same as the front dining room but here, Natalie had painted the oblong plaster mouldings on the walls white with a delicate blue-green moss shade for the background. Below the dado rail the wood panels had become scuffed and scratched over the years by all the junk that had been stored there, probably from long before David and his wife had moved in. Since they had never used the room for anything else, he was more than happy for Natalie to sand and paint the wood a darker tone of the moss-coloured shade above.

"Wow! You've been really busy. Where on earth have you found the time? You'll be exhausted." Stephen placed his arm around her shoulders.

"It's been difficult. Dad has done a bit, but I've done most of it so far. It's taking a while."

"May I help out?" Stephen asked.

They were still treading around each other carefully. Natalie was extremely tired. Her eyes were stinging and her limbs heavy. "I'd love some help," she said.

He enfolded her in his arms and simply held her close. It was all she wanted at that moment. She breathed more easily when wrapped in his familiar warmth and scent.

Her voice was small and muffled by his chest as she said, "I'm still desperate to find my mother. Not to rub her nose in my success, but to share it and reassure her that I'm okay and have a wonderful family. She must have suffered."

CHAPTER 40

Contented and warm, Maggie lay in Rick St George's bed, with one of his arms across her stomach. Her mind wandered over all the things she had become and all the things for which she was so grateful.

Rick had responded to her story with sensitivity and love. "You must have a low opinion of me if you think I can't empathise with the desperation in which you found yourself, even if it's difficult to understand fully because I've never been in that situation. You clearly have had an even lower opinion of yourself, but you've overcome huge things in your life. It's the different thickness of threads in the weave of a single life that makes us who we are. It's made you the person I love and of whom I'm so proud."

The sun behind the curtains grew brighter, sliding across the duvet cover and up the wall. Still they lay, relaxed and satisfied.

Maggie sighed. "I could stay here all day, but I do need to get up and go and get some milk before I go home. The shop will be closed again at this rate."

Rick moved his arm as he rolled over. "Of course, if you moved here permanently, it wouldn't be a problem. I have milk, you know."

"Yes," she said.

He sat up and the covers fell away to reveal the torso with which she had become so familiar. "Yes?"

"Yes, I could move in with you."

His chin fell to his chest, a great gust of air left his body, and his shoulders sank.

"What? What's the matter?" It was her turn to sit up. "Don't you want me now?"

"Oh, you! Of course I do. I've waited such a long time, and I can't believe you've agreed. At last. Come here." Rick put both arms around her and despite the awkwardness of their sideways positions, his embrace was all she needed and wanted. As they fell back against the pillows, he kissed her roundly and she was only too pleased to accept him a second time that morning.

Maggie had the strong desire to skip around her little house later that day, as she planned what she would take with her and what she would be happy to sell. She and Rick had roughly discussed selling both houses and finding one together. They would start afresh with everything shared and equal. It would take time, of course, and in the meantime she would live at his house, where there was a little more space.

As Maggie stood at the sink, the doorbell sounded, making her jump. She wasn't expecting anyone, unless Rick simply couldn't stay away. She grinned. *I probably look like a loon*, she thought, but the grin left her face as she opened the door.

The face was immediately recognisable. The blonde hair was shorter and cut well, with artful highlights and lowlights. The clothes were classic rather than the latest fashion, but the wearer stood tall and straight, which added to their overall elegance.

Maggie's knees trembled. Just when her life seemed too good, this was coming back to haunt her. A thousand scenarios flew through her brain.

"Harriet," she managed to croak.

"Maggie, it is you. I've searched from time to time but now with the internet, things are so much easier. As time has gone on, I've become more and more consumed by curiosity."

All that Maggie could think after the initial wave of shock was, *I look a wreck.* She scraped her hand through her hair.

"Can I come in? You look like you've seen a ghost." Harriet laughed.

Even the laugh and diction were different, yet this was definitely Harriet. Maggie stood back without a word as Harriet passed her with a strong waft of something expensive.

She gathered her senses. "On the right." She indicated the door to the sitting room.

"What a lovely little place this is," Harriet said, and Maggie was instantly aware of its smallness and its lack of expensive glassware, or pictures, or ... anything, really. She was transported back to being that insecure and worried girl she was before, even though Harriet had been her friend and champion.

They sat opposite each other, and still Maggie couldn't speak.

"I can see I've shocked you," Harriet said. "I should have texted or emailed or something, but I haven't found that sort of info. I got your address through a right convoluted way, using electoral roll and other stuff. Lucky you never changed your name." Harriet stood up. "Shall we have a cup of tea or something? That always used to help, didn't it?"

"Oh yes, sorry." Maggie shot in front of her. "You wait here. I'll get it. Tea or coffee?"

When she returned with a tray, Harriet was standing and looking out of the window. Again, Maggie was insecure about the high-density housing area in which she lived.

"It's part of a New Township, this place. Not everyone's favourite, but it's been okay," she said and realised she sounded apologetic.

Harriet made no comment but came and sat down, and Maggie passed her a mug of tea.

"Look…" Harriet said.

"I need…" Maggie spoke at the same time.

"Let's start again," Harriet said. "Just tell me why. I've worried about you over the years, you know, I really have."

This time, the story came a little more easily. Having unburdened her soul to Rick, Maggie was tempted to make something up, but this woman had always been her friend.

Harriet sat impassively and listened. There was no flicker of emotion and certainly no judgement. Eventually, she asked, "But why leave? I'd have understood all that. We'd have managed, together, somehow."

This was it. Somehow, instinct told Maggie she had to discover the truth if her life with Rick was ever going to work. Her fingers twisted and her throat closed before she took a deep breath and tried to still her racing heart.

"I was frightened of what had happened to Jay. That it wasn't an accident and that…"

"You've thought Billy had a hand in it. I can see the question on your face. Well, let me tell you." She paused. "Back when that all happened, I only saw him very occasionally by then. I was never totally sure either, to be honest. Do you remember Billy said it'd all work out, after I told him? That's it, isn't it? He did always look out for me when I used to see him and his mates regularly, and I was never sure if he had a hand in the accident. I guess we'll never know. I didn't see him again, Maggie. The police coming round that time scared me witless, if I'm honest."

"What? Never? You didn't see him again?"

"Nope. It wasn't all that long after you disappeared, a few months, that I heard on the grapevine that he ended up inside for something else."

"Something else? What something else? When you say inside, you mean prison?"

"Exactly. He was involved in all sorts, I guess, and I heard he was part of a gang that got caught for knifing some guy outside a pub. I don't know the details and I've never wanted to know."

"You told me at the time 'these things have a way of being okay'. The next thing I knew, Jay was killed in an accident — just like his parents were. I was so scared, I ran for it, then everything went wrong. Harriet, I thought you might be involved, and I fled. I'm so sorry."

"It sounds like you paid the price so, the way I see it, you have nothing to be sorry about, hun."

Maggie needed a break. "This tea's gone cold. I'll make another one." She gathered up the mugs and escaped to the kitchen.

"Don't run away again, hun."

Maggie turned from gripping the front of the sink, to see Harriet standing in the doorway. "Oh, Harriet. You've always watched out for me, helped me in untold ways with unstinting generosity and I've let you down."

"There you go again, always putting yourself in the bad slot. Listen, I don't know if Billy was involved — but if he was, it's divine retribution that he's been inside all these years."

"If he's out again by now, does that mean he'll come looking for you or anything?"

"No. It won't happen. Be sure of that. I go by my married name, although I'm divorced." Harriet shrugged and counted on her fingers. "That's one thing and it's another tale. Let me finish this one first. Two, I've moved house that many times, and three, I'm living in Peterborough now — so nowhere near, and nothing to do with back then. I'm in a good job. I've changed my life, too."

"Peterborough! Wow! Coincidence or what? We better take this tea and go through and catch up properly," Maggie said.

"Not such a huge coincidence. Shall I carry this?" Harriet picked up her mug and headed back to the little sitting room.

Once seated, Maggie didn't know where to begin. "So how did you find me?" she asked.

"Once, I started searching, it wasn't so hard. I looked on the electoral roll because I couldn't find you on social media at all."

Maggie smiled and shrugged. "No, I've steered clear of social media.."

"If you really want to disappear, you need to change your name, hun," Harriet said.

"So how come you're in Peterborough out of all the places to choose?"

"I came because the company came initially. So many did back in the eighties. I came ten years later."

"You've been in this region all that time?"

"Yep. We could have bumped into each other in Queensgate at any time." Harriet sipped her tea and Maggie looked at her over the rim of her own mug.

"I don't go into the city that much," Maggie said. "Where are you living? Are you with anyone?"

"We, that's John and I, live in Waterthorpe. We've got a house we had built. I'd like to have bought one of the old stone cottages, but he said it would be too much like hard work. He's probably right. He has a head for finances, works at Lynch Wood Business Park."

"I work there now. Where is he?"

"He's in ad marketing."

"No! That's where my friend Rick works. It's a massive place, I suppose. Over two thousand employees."

"They've probably passed each other at some point or sat near each other at lunchtime." Harriet giggled. "Changing the subject, let's address the elephant in the corner."

"Which one?" Maggie said. "I think there's a herd?"

"The child."

"Ah."

"Have you found her? Have you been in touch?"

"No."

"That article in the local paper." Harriet's face showed Maggie she had almost pieced things together but still wasn't certain. "Is that you?"

Maggie looked at her fingers as they wound together in her lap.

"Maggie, you can't leave it like that." Harriet glanced at her watch. "Oh no, I have to go. I said I'd meet John from work. We're going to the cinema. Why don't you come? We'll go for something to eat after."

"No, but thanks anyway."

"Look, I only work part-time. I've got tomorrow off, so why don't we meet up for a coffee? Oh, I suppose you have to work."

"I could leave early. Where should we go?"

"There's a teashop, Tea and Sweet Dreams, at Moondreams House. Do you know it?"

"I've been there a couple of times. It's lovely, and the lass who runs it seems really friendly. I could meet you there at four?"

Harriet giggled again. "It's amazing we haven't bumped into each other. That's on the edge of my village."

By this time, they were standing at Maggie's front door. "See you tomorrow, then." Harriet looked at her watch again. "Must fly." She turned and blew a kiss as she hurried towards her car.

CHAPTER 41

The newspaper was on the only free table in the teashop when Maggie and Harriet arrived. There was a gentle murmur of voices and one or two people nodded at Maggie as she took her seat. The knitting ladies had mostly dispersed, and only one or two remained. Maggie moved the paper onto the low window ledge next to her, with as much casual nonchalance as she could muster. She wanted no reminders of that today.

"What shall we have? Is it too early for a glass of wine?"

Seeing the paper had unsettled Maggie, but she managed a smile and agreed that wine was called for. "After all," she said, "it's a celebration of sorts, isn't it?"

"It is indeed. Do you have Pinot Grigio?" she asked the waitress when she came over.

"It's Ellie, isn't it?" Maggie said.

"Yes, that's right. Is it the same for you both?"

"Yes, please." Her daughter would be older than this lass, Maggie thought. Older, blonde, probably. Would she be married? Have a family of her own? Her thoughts wandered on.

When the wine glasses and a small bowl of olives arrived, she took a draught of the cool, clear liquid and tried to switch off those thoughts, as she had a million times before.

Harriet smiled at her, reached across the small table and touched her arm. "You live with it, don't you? The wondering. Probably guilt as well, if I know anything about you."

Maggie nodded. "It's affected so many things in my life, but Rick has been the best thing to happen since … since I gave birth. And I think we can make it work. At last."

Natalie came through from the other room and seeing the pair, she walked across. "Good afternoon, ladies. Do you have everything you need?"

"Oh, yes, thank you," Harriet said.

"I'm so pleased I discovered this place," Maggie added. "You've created something exceedingly special here."

The last two knitting ladies stood to leave. "See you next time, perhaps?" one of them said to Maggie.

"Absolutely. Thank you."

"Thank you. Goodnight." Natalie smiled at them and then returned her attention to Maggie with an even wider grin. "You've made my day. When I first started out, it was to try and impress someone in particular, but I've no need to do that now."

"Oh?"

"Tell us more," Harriet said in her customary forthright way, which hadn't altered over the years.

Natalie looked sheepish, Maggie thought.

"Well … if you could pass me that newspaper. Sorry, I left it there earlier. I sat here in the sun when the place was empty and grabbed a quick cuppa. I'll show you."

Before Maggie could think how to change the subject, Harriet passed the newspaper containing the article. Natalie unfolded it and held the article for the two friends to see.

There was the damning headline in bold letters and a whole page devoted to the story: *Still Searching for her Mother.* There was the grainy photograph of the bag Maggie had used, the note she had written, and a full exposé of her crime.

Natalie continued, "It was this lady. I've been searching for her, and at one time I was cross and unforgiving. But now I know she must have been desperate, and I know there is absolutely nothing to forgive. They said they'd do another next week with my photograph as I am…"

Maggie was certain the blood must have left her heart entirely. She was unable to croak a response, unable to move, unable to breathe.

"Are you alright? Can I get you something?" Natalie had realised she looked ill.

Harriet stood and put her arms around her friend. "She's had a shock. She'll be alright." Then she whispered in Maggie's ear, "You have to say something. You must tell her."

Maggie shot a glance at Natalie before she looked away again.

Natalie's frown of puzzlement deepened, and then she sat with a thump in Harriet's empty chair. "Are you … oh … you're not, are you?"

Harriet looked at Maggie and must have seen something in her friend's expression, because she turned to Natalie and nodded before she said, "That's about the size of it."

Natalie's voice came out like a rasp. "You're this lady? The one I'm searching for?"

"I'm sorry. I'm so ashamed and so sorry," Maggie managed to say. She couldn't look up.

"I can't believe it," Natalie said. "At last. I hardly dare believe it. There is nothing to be sorry about. I've found you. After all this time. And in my very own tea shop. What could be better? I can't believe … oh!" She stretched out her hand but couldn't reach Maggie.

Harriet took it. "You have no idea why, or what she went through, I imagine."

Natalie shook her head, unable to say more.

"Come and sit together on that settee," Harriet said. Brooking no argument, she raised Maggie and supported her as she crossed the room.

Natalie rose, too, and went to sit on the dark red, leather seat by the wall. "Really, there is nothing to be sorry about," she said and touched Maggie's arm as they sat in close proximity. There was warmth in her voice, and Maggie looked up at last.

"I'm off to the ladies' loo. I need to touch up my … something, whatever," Harriet said. She gave a chuckle and hastened away.

"Are you my mother? This lady who must have been so desperate to do such a brave thing as this?" Natalie still clutched the newspaper.

Maggie nodded. She had to tell all. This was the opportunity for her final act of redemption. She must summon her courage as she had done before, so many times. If her child could not accept her and what she had done, at least she would have been honest at last, and she could go to Rick with the truth. Surely this was a chance for her to begin her life.

And so it came out. All of it. Near the end, they were both in tears. Natalie leapt up at one point and grabbed long pieces of blue kitchen roll from behind her counter. They laughed, they cried some more, they clung to each other.

"My parents, well, my dad has been amazing." Natalie explained her situation. "I'm so lucky to have him, and my upbringing has been as happy as any could be. Me and my mum get on better now, too. I like her husband well enough."

Harriet reappeared. "I see things seem to be alright." Both Maggie and Natalie nodded. "I'll be off. Give me a call," she said to Maggie, who leapt up to give her a hug.

It wasn't long before William arrived. "I forgot the time," Natalie said. "Dad, you'll never believe who this is."

Maggie slunk into the settee. Guilt and shame and upset gripped her again.

When introductions were made, William said, "I have you to thank, do I? You gave me your child. What greater gift is there than that? How unimaginably brave you must have been."

Maggie stood. He took both her hands in his and kissed each cheek with warm, dry lips. Maggie was so grateful, she could have burst into song.

Then the door opened again. All eyes turned as Stephen walked in. "Oh, hello, William. I hadn't realised you were coming for our girl." He pushed his heavy hair from his brow. "I came to collect you, Nats." Then he frowned. "Are you okay? Have you been crying?" He came and put his arm around her, and she leaned into him as he looked from one to the other. They all smiled.

"What was lost is now found," Natalie said, looking up at him, "and here, too, at Moondreams House where dreams do come true. I'll tell you about it, but it's a long story, my love."

A NOTE TO THE READER

Dear Reader,

I've set this story in and around Moondreams House and I hope you have enjoyed meeting again some of the characters from the first book in the series. Some of the action also occurs in Peterborough, a city with which I am very familiar and is worth visiting for the hidden gem of the cathedral. The city has changed a huge amount since Maggie arrived there, but local people will recognise many of the shops and streets she passed along. Any minor changes I made or differences you spot are for the purposes of the plot but they are few. I was very careful to research the city layout for the time frame of Maggie's arrival.

My thanks again go the team at Sapere Books for their cover design, editing, and marketing expertise. Without them, I as a writer, and you as a reader, would have missed much.

If you enjoyed reading *Lost and Found*, perhaps you might leave a brief review on **Amazon** or **Goodreads**. It doesn't need to be long; a couple of sentences will more than suffice. It will inform readers when choosing a book and would be a huge boost to this author. Thank you.

If you would like to know more about my writing, my website is **www.rosrendleauthor.co.uk**. Here you can also **sign up for my newsletter** where I often offer free gifts and timely access and information about forthcoming books. I'd love to hear from you, my dear reader, and you are able to chat with me via **Facebook** or via **Twitter.**

Thank you, again, and I hope we will meet soon through the pages of one of my other books.

Ros Rendle

Sapere Books is an exciting new publisher of brilliant fiction and popular history.

To find out more about our latest releases and our monthly bargain books visit our website:
saperebooks.com

www.ingramcontent.com/pod-product-compliance
Lightning Source LLC
Chambersburg PA
CBHW060432180626
46817CB00007B/2772